VENOLA THE VEGETARIAN

VENOLA
THE VEGETARIAN

Cheryl Ware

Charleston, West Virginia

Quarrier Press
Charleston, WV

Cover and illustrations: Tanner M. Rainey
Book design: Mark S. Phillips

Paperback:
ISBN 13: 978-1-891852-57-2
ISBN 10: 1-891852-57-4

Library of Congress Control Number: 2008923245

10 9 8 7 6 5 4 3 2

Printed in the United States of America

Distributed by:

West Virginia Book Co.
1125 Central Ave.
Charleston, WV 25302

www.wvbookco.com

DEDICATION

In memory of Gary Bookout, whose wit, intelligence,
and compassion combined to form the perfect teacher!

Thanks to all my Venolas:
Debbie Benedetti, Mariah and Nancy Bennett, Elizabeth Campbell,
Cindy and Wayne Martin, Barbie Miller, Marsa Myers,
Robert Price, Abby and Sharon Reese, Stephanie Runion,
Sandy Vrana, and Rebecca Wallace.
You each added something very unique
to Venola's latest adventure!

Wednesday, April 19

Dear Journal,

I hate breakfast, but my parents insist. They call it "a brain booster." Eating too early makes me feel gross, especially if Mama is frying sausage or eggs. But since she's been pregnant, she hasn't been forcing big fried breakfasts on anyone. Thanks, Morning Sickness! Mostly it's whatever we can find for ourselves like cold cereal or toast, which even *my* weak stomach can handle.

The only thing I miss is my all-time favorite breakfast food— chocolate pudding! When I complained, Mama said, "If you want it, there's the stove. You're old enough to fix it yourself." Who wants to wake up in time to do that? This baby isn't even here and is already turning my life upside down.

When I first heard the news, I wasn't crazy about a baby invading my space. After all, what seventh grader wants to be followed around by a little copycat? But now I'm sort of looking forward to the big day—if the baby is a girl. Although my parents are stubborn and say they don't want to know if they are having a boy or girl, I'm bugging them because I ABSOLUTELY HAVE TO KNOW before I burst into a bazillion little pieces. They don't have as much at stake in this as I do. I have FOUR brothers, so I need another sister to help even things out. Mama says, "A baby is a baby."

Yeah, right. She's just hoping she can use our old baby clothes, and she has more for boys. I told her the other night, "If you *promise* to have a girl, I'll buy new clothes with my paper route money." I was *just* making a joke and trying to get Mama to slip up—just in case she knows the sex of the baby, but Dad, who was listening in to our discussion, didn't catch on to my trickery.

"It doesn't work like that, Darlin'," he said, mussing my hair, which I absolutely hate. "Your mother can't make you any promises. That matter was decided months ago. Almost six to be exact." He winked at Mama.

Does he think I'm an idiot? After all, I do take general science and health class. "*Yes*, Dad," I said, "Thanks to Mr. Bookout's chromosome lesson, I know who's to blame if I get a brother." I straightened my hair the best I could without a mirror. "So expect a lousy Father's Day present if you bring home another boy."

Dad muttered, "What are they teaching in today's schools?" and then he walked off to find wrestling on TV.

Four brothers are plenty. Technically, I have a sister, too, but she is as old as the hills and barely worth counting. Nineteen. Katrina wants nothing to do with me and spends her time doing three things. 1. Going out with friends, usually to buy clothes. 2. Working at Pizza Hut. 3. Talking on the phone about going out with friends and Pizza Hut. Bor-ing.

Sometimes getting a call through to my best friend is next to impossible. Last night I needed to talk with Sally, but I never got a chance before her bedtime. I told Mama she should invent an impartial system so *all* her children can use the telephone equally, but she said, "I have enough to do without playing phone monitor, too. I have raised intelligent children who can compromise and get along with each other."

I do not know where these mystery children of hers live, but I hope they don't move in with the rest of us. We're too crowded as it is.

P.S. Why did Dad say Mama can't make me any promises about the baby being a girl? Does he already know it's a boy? Ahhhh!

P.P.S. Once the baby gets here, will Mama go back to making my pudding?

Thursday, April 20

Dear Journal,

I made an earthshaking decision today. At first, I was just grossed out in science class, and I vowed never to touch raw meat again, but the more I thought about the experiment, the more it bugged me, so this is my vow: I, Venola Mae Cutright, from this day forth, am a full-fledged vegetarian. NO MORE MEAT!

We had already dissected a frog this year, so I didn't think anything could out disgust that, but today in science lab, Mr. Bookout passed out toothpicks. He made a big deal about us washing our hands, and then said, "Okay, class, listen carefully. I would like you to take your toothpick, and *gently* scrape the inside of your OWN cheek. Not too deep. And do not, I repeat do *not*, use the toothpick for any other purpose than instructed. I don't want to have to interrupt class to call an ambulance for any impaled students, and I do not want to have to call any parents and inform them as to why their child prodigy has been shishkabobbed in general science class." He always laughs like he is the funniest comedian on earth. He is NOT the funniest comedian on earth. No one laughs at his jokes except Missy Fowler who sits up front and tries to rack up brownie points because she is lousy at science.

Anyway, we swiped our toothpicks across the insides of our cheeks, and then wiped the slime on the slides and examined it under microscopes. Mr. Bookout explained that our bodies are made of cells, and it was combination cool/weird to think about the inside of my body squirming around. I thought about how many times I had bitten the inside of my cheeks by accident and swallowed my own squiggly cells. Ugh. Does that make me part cannibal?

If that wasn't enough, next Mr. Bookout brought out some slimy, raw hamburger and made a big production of everyone smearing some on a clean slide. All the squirmy action under the microscope made me queasier than watching my brother Bobby pour his glass of milk in his chicken noodle soup. Bobby says it all ends up in the same place anyway.

I looked up at the shelves of dead things Mr. Bookout has floating in jars of formaldehyde and, for some reason, felt myself getting hot and then cold. Goosebumps shot out everywhere, and my arms had little droplets of water coming out of every pore. Sweat was running off my forehead, and my heart was beating way too fast. I even felt sweat dripping off the backs of my knees.

Worst of all, Mr. Practical Joker Bookout arranged his lesson to complement lunchroom cuisine. What else? Hamburger Day. Most of us threw the burgers straight in the trash and survived on fries and fruit cocktail. I love fries more than anything else in the world, and I usually get extras from my always-on-a-diet, weight-conscious friends, even though we're not supposed to share or trade food. However, thanks to Mr. Bookout, people at my table were hanging on to their fries like they were gold. Fruit cocktail doesn't have a very high exchange rate on the school lunch black market, but sometimes you can get a pretty decent pile of fries for a hamburger. Not today!

I don't mind that Mr. Bookout caused me to make a life-changing decision because I've never been that crazy about meat, but when he ruins French Fry Day, I say, "Growl to Mr. Bookout!"

\I
⌃

P.S. I'm going to talk Sally into being a vegetarian, too. Surfing the net for vegetarian recipes will be more fun without a flesh eater beside me.

Thursday, April 20 evening

Dear Journal,

   I told Mama I am now a vegetarian, and she put down her fork and took a break from talking about how sleepy being pregnant is making her. She said, "Oh no, you are not, Young Lady." Does she think I am three? If I hadn't made my announcement, would she even have noticed my eating habits have changed? How many times can one woman mention a baby that's not even here yet? Sometimes it's all I can do to keep from plugging my ears with my fingers when she starts one of the "B-A-B-Y" stories.

   Luckily, I didn't announce my decision until supper was almost over, and all the sloppy joes had been gobbled up by my four older brothers.

   My supper consisted of cornbread, brown beans, boiled potatoes, and chocolate pudding. Not bad for my first day as a vegetarian.

From: "Venola" <cutright1@mtnbelle.net>
To: "Sally" <scathell@mtnbelle.net>
Subject: Veggie Pact
Date: Thursday, April 20; Time 21:07

Sally,
Will you be a vegetarian with me?
Venola the Vegetarian

From: "Venola" <cutright1@mtnbelle.net>
To: "Sally" <scathell@mtnbelle.net>
Subject: Veggie Pact
Date: Thursday, April 20; Time 21:19

S.,
Yes, I'll still eat at your table, even if you are a flesh eater! Ha. Ha. And definitely you may have my fish sticks. Can I have some of your Tater Tots?

P.S. Either way, you can still have my dead fish.

Love,
V. the V.

Friday evening, April 21

Dear Journal,

Mayday. Mama says we are *all* going to the City Park for the Annual International Ramp Festival and Cook-off tomorrow. I've read about some of the weird recipes, like "ramp crepes" or "ramp lasagna" in the newspaper, but I didn't think normal people actually went to such a thing. Mama said, "We need to celebrate our West Virginia heritage. Where's your state pride and spirit?"

I say, if ramps are the best we can do for state pride, it's time to pack up and move to Ohio.

I have never eaten a ramp, which is about five thousand times stinkier than a regular onion, but I've smelled them seeping out of my classmates' pores this week. Gag! It was so bad, Mrs. Montgomery turned us into icicles by opening the windows even though it was freezing out. Plus, she sprayed floral disinfectant which just made it even harder to breathe! Then when she was dismissing us today, she offered us extra-credit points for not eating them over the weekend! So you know it's bad if a teacher's giving away extra-credit!

My two oldest brothers, James and Philip, weaseled out of going by having to work, but Bobby, Melvin, and I can't get out of it no matter what excuses we try. My personal attempts at a reprieve include claiming a spelling test, a science presentation to prepare for, and a track meet. Nothing works.

Dad said, "They'll have normal grub for us non-rampers. And when did *you* take up track?" It's hard to pull anything over on Dad because unfortunately for me, he doesn't have as severe a case of baby-on-the-brain as my mother.

My older sister didn't even need an excuse. She just flatly refused. Being the oldest has benefits. I think if Katrina came home and said, "Mom, Dad, I committed a bank robbery," they would say, "That's nice, Dear. Venola, don't make me tell you again to wash those dishes!" Maybe once the baby comes and I'm not the youngest, I'll get away with more, too. Come *on*, baby!

Saturday, April 22

Dear Journal,

Perhaps the ramp fumes went to my brain because I had a great time at the festival. Sally went with us, so I didn't have to endure an entire afternoon with Bobby and Melvin.

A really cute artist was painting ramps on people's faces, so I dared Sally into getting a little cartoon ramp on her cheek.

"I'll pay," I said.

She walked right over and plopped down! "I was getting ready to pay myself, just to have an excuse to talk to him," she said.

He was an expert at flirting with his customers, which definitely helped sell his ramp-art. Sally, convinced he was in love with her, said it was the best thing we'd ever spent money on. Not that *she* spent money on it. Then, she made me get painted too, so that she could flirt longer.

After *we* spent all *my* money, we spotted my parents eating in a big tent.

"I'm starving," I said.

Mama offered me a bite of her chicken, but I shook my head. She is still trying to force me into eating things with faces.

Dad offered me a bite of his fried potatoes. Without thinking, I opened my mouth and swallowed. Everyone burst out laughing.

"There better not have been anything with a face mixed in with those!" I said, ready to start gagging.

Dad guffawed harder. "Nope, not unless you count the potatoes. They do have eyes, right?"

Bobby blurted out, "RAMPS! You just ate the things you've been ranting about all morning. What a hypocrite!"

Ahhh! Somehow when I had my head turned, my dad had gone over to the smelly side and taken me with him. Since I was already a stinker, I let Sally talk me into sharing ramp bread. So who knows, maybe we'll be the two stinkiest people on the bus!

I guess I can kiss Mrs. Montgomery's extra-credit goodbye.

Sunday, April 23

Dear Journal,

I cannot make out ramp breath on myself, although Bobby insists I'm a walking ramp-bomb.

Mama ate raw ramps at the festival, which is the worst, and actually thought she could cover up the all-powerful fumes. Right before we left for church this morning, she doused herself in about a half bottle of perfume. Then, down the bumpy, windy road we went.

Since it was colder than usual, my parents turned on the heater. The perfume and the ramps started floating and mixing around the inside of the car until I was pretty much convinced it was toxic. They also refused to roll down the car windows, no matter how much the rest of us complained. Mama said, "You'll catch a cold and have to miss school with a sore throat."

I tried to tell her this would be an added bonus so as not to have to smell my rampy classmates, but Mama gave me the "Enough" look, and I shut up because believe you me, Mama mad is not a pretty sight. So I suffered the rest of the way in silence, trying not to throw up, while my chicken-hearted brother Bobby giggled and made gagging faces behind Mama's back.

I got even once we were at church. I zoomed in and grabbed the aisle seat in our pew, latching on to that wood tighter than a termite. Bobby tried to bulldoze me into scooting down by sitting on my lap, but Mama dragged him by the arm, all the way to the other end of the pew. She forced him to sit between her and Dad to make sure he behaved. I've never seen him as pale green as when he was sandwiched between our parents, holding the hymnal as Mama belted out a rampy rendition of "Nearer, My God, to Thee." I think God better let the ramps wear off before He lets her take a step closer to Him! Tee hee.

P.S. Never buy your mother perfume because you like the pretty bottle.

Monday, April 24

Dear Journal,

No one at school smelled me, or at least no one said anything to my face.

But then my favorite customer, Miss Wilma Facemeir, said, "Hi, Stinky," when I stopped by the funeral home to deliver her paper. I put my hand up and blew to test my breath. Then I spotted the Shop-N-Save grocery bags on her kitchen table and realized Bobby had made a delivery and put her up to teasing me.

P.S. Mama says the baby has been karate-chopping more than usual.

"Those butterflies fluttering around inside me are starting to feel more like kangaroos jumping. Feel," she said. Even though it gives me the creeps, I put my hand where she indicated. I couldn't feel a thing besides the regular up and down of her breathing.

"Mama, if she's upset and kicking, it's your fault."

"What did I do?" she asked.

"Well, you said babies develop their five senses way before they are born. I'd kick, too, if you put me in a dark place and force-fed me ramps. My poor defenseless sister doesn't even have a window in there to open." Mama just laughed and said to go clean my pigsty.

As I got up to leave, I said, "Hey, I'm just saying that some might consider eating ramps child abuse."

Mama pointed down the hallway to my room which I admit is in need of an intervention or a team of Merry Maids. Ever since I became a vegetarian, I spend all my time reading about how to survive without meat, which I think is a lot more important than having a clean room. I wonder if other vegetarians are slobs, too.

"And by the way," Mama yelled after me. "Quit calling the baby, your 'sister.' *Hearing* is also one of the five senses, and there is a

50/50 chance you are riling up your little brother every time you call him a girl."

Touché, Mama! Touché! Miss Wilma says the reason Mama and I fuss is we are too much alike, which is ridiculous. Yes, we would both rather curl up and read a book than clean and we both enjoy getting the last word in. But still!

(If the baby is a brother, getting the first word in and making him mad before he's even born is an added bonus, don't you think?)

Monday, April 24

Dear Journal,

Why does Mama always jump to conclusions and blame Miss Wilma when I get a new idea that she doesn't approve of? Miss Wilma is my eccentric retired teacher friend who lives over the funeral home. I met her when I started my paper route last summer, and we have talked almost every day since.

"How could Miss Wilma cause ME to be a vegetarian, Mama? She loves meat more than I love chocolate!" I said.

"I don't know about her antics sometimes!" Mama said. Ever since I announced that Miss Wilma and I were going to be cremated when we died, Mama has been weary of Miss Wilma's influence on me.

When I told Miss Wilma she was in trouble with my mother AGAIN, she said, "Girl, do you have to blab everything you know?" Then she pretty much said that I should keep my big fat mouth shut if I want any more of her brownies and stories. I'm trying!

It seems like everyone in town is jealous because this 84-year-old lady is one of my best friends. Unlike Sally, who sometimes insinuates that I'm not girly enough because I don't think about my hair and weight 24/7, Miss Wilma just accepts me as I am. I don't seem to get on Miss Wilma's nerves like I do other people's. Also, she bakes fattening desserts, gossips, watches TV, and even lets me listen to rock and roll, as long as it doesn't rattle the boom-box completely off her countertop. Who wouldn't want a friend like this?

Grandma thinks if I am spending time with an older person, I should come to her house, but she and I don't have much in common, although Sally does tease me that I'm on my way to becoming her because I have one cat and feed every stray that I see. Ha. Ha. I couldn't find enough strays to catch up with Granny. She is a dozen ahead of me—at last count.

Sally resents Miss Wilma, too. When I ask her to hang out or go to the movies, she makes snide remarks, such as, "Are you sure you can drag yourself away from Miss Wilma for two hours?" So you can see, I have to remember not to mention Miss Wilma to the rest of the world too often. But she is so funny! She tells the best stories about her crazy brother who owns the funeral home in which she lives, and like I said, I have FOUR extremely crazy brothers myself, and the threat of another one on the way, so I can relate big time!

When her brother, Mr. Facemeir, left her apartment yesterday, I asked Miss Wilma why he wears glow-in-the-dark white socks with his fancy dark funeral home suits. "Maybe you could clue him in that it's not cool," I suggested. "He looks like he just stepped out of a J.C. Penney catalog, and then he goes and ruins the look."

"He's worn ugly white tube socks since he was old enough to shop for himself." She started giggling and shaking her head from side to side.

"No fair! What's so funny?" I begged.

"Oh, I was just thinking of Johnny as a child. He was such a little control freak that he numbered his white socks with a black marker, so he could match them up easier."

"Why white socks?" I asked, not fully grasping the concept.

"He couldn't see the numbers when he marked dark socks, and white markers rubbed off. I always suspected the reason he numbered them at all was he knew none of us would steal a pair with numbers as big as tarantulas across the toes. He denies it to this day and says he just wants his socks to wear out evenly."

"He *still* numbers them?"

"I'm surprised you never noticed with your eagle eyes," she said. "Yes, we finally just came to accept the little nut and his idiosyncrasies.

"In fact, he converted some friends in sixth grade. But when they started dating, their girlfriends put a stop to the Sock Club

15

quicker than you can eat a pan of my brownies. Mother said it was just a phase! Boy, was she wrong."

"How do sisters ever live in the same house with their weirdo brothers?" I asked. "Didn't you want to change your address without telling him?"

"At the time, I wanted Mother to have him committed, but other than the obvious fashion violation, it isn't too bad except when he takes off his shoes in front of company. People unaware of his 'system' often think he's an escaped convict!"

"You are just making that up," I said, snorting so hard that chocolate milk squirted out my nose.

"Wait until he stops by. I'll tell him I just scrubbed the floor and to take his shoes off, and you can see Mr. Chain Gang's feet for yourself."

It was good to hear Miss Wilma calling her brother "Johnny" and sharing funny family memories. Mostly, she just fumes because he bosses her around. Maybe there is hope for Bobby and me. Miss Wilma is 84, and I am almost 13. Let's see, that gives me only 71 short years to learn to like my most annoying brother. I might as well give up now.

When I came back into the living room with a paper towel for my chocolate milk mishap, I asked, "Why don't you buy him some dark socks?"

"Oh, he has plenty. He's just saving them 'for good.' Don't ever live that way, Venola. Enjoy whatever you have the moment you get it, and if you use it all up, treasure the memory until you can get some more."

Then she pulled a can of freshly baked cookies out from under the coffee table, and we practiced what she preached.

P.S. How can anyone get mad at Miss Wilma? She never once mentioned the word "vegetarian" to me! Mr. Bookout is the one who grossed me out with the slides, cells, bacteria, and meat. Maybe Mama should let me drop out of school before he ruins me completely. Or at least out of general science class.

P.P.S. Then again, Miss Wilma and I *have* been talking about *bad* cells lately. The doctors are running some pretty serious tests on her, but I am trying not to think about it. Plus, she has sworn me to secrecy. The only reason she told me at all is I overheard her scheduling an appointment. I am good at talking people into sharing details. Mama calls it "wearing her down," which I suppose is what happened to Miss Wilma.

Finally, she just blurted out, "Stop badgering me. The hospital needs some extra money this month, so they want to do a biopsy." Then she went into the kitchen and started making a triple-layer German chocolate cake with coconut-pecan icing.

I can barely breathe for thinking about her upcoming test. What if she does have breast cancer? Could she survive at her age?

Tuesday, April 25

Dear Journal,

Being a vegetarian is going to be easy. I do not like the smell of most meats cooking or frying. The three I am going to miss are bacon, pepperoni, and rotisserie chicken. Crunchy things don't seem like they are from animals. Doesn't pepperoni seem more like a spicy, crunchy potato chip than an animal?

Oh well. I am lucky that all of my other favorite foods are vegetarian.

Favorite foods:

1. French fries
2. Potato chips
3. Doritos
4. Grilled cheese sandwiches
5. Homemade rolls and bread (with lots of butter!)
6. Chocolate pudding
7. Chocolate ice cream
8. Chocolate candy
9. Jolly Ranchers
10. Mashed potatoes

P.S. I also like Dr. Pepper, but does it count as a food?

Wednesday, April 26

Dear Journal,

Today was an okay lunch day. The cooks fixed meatloaf, which I never eat anyway because it is squishy and a little pink in the middle. However, I do fine because I love #5 and #10 on my food list, and they always serve these as sides. The cooks may not be the best, but they are dependable.

On meatloaf day, I have a running "date" with Sammy Potter. He slips me his hot roll, and I pass him my meatloaf. We have to be sly and pass when no teachers or narcky students are looking because no one is allowed to trade food since Tommy Flint almost exploded trying to set a record by eating everyone's hot dogs. He was up to 23 when he was caught. The school administration sent him to the emergency room, but I think he would have kept eating until he popped if a teacher hadn't noticed kids crowding around his table, yelling, "Go! Go! Go!"

"No sharing" is a goofy elementary rule, which we are way too old for, but I guess teachers have to do whatever is necessary to keep students from exploding. Parents would probably sue.

Speaking of childish rules, you'll never believe this. Because our lunchroom is so noisy, Mr. Bookout says the junior high might adopt our old elementary "silent for the first fifteen minutes of lunch" rule. I hope this is just one of his jokes. I hated that rule because when I wasn't allowed to talk, I got my best ideas. Then I never failed getting caught trying to share them. I felt like I would explode, just like Tommy Flint! So to keep this from happening, I just *had* to talk. That's why I spent a lot of my early years sitting by the cranky teacher who was stuck with year-round lunch duty. She wouldn't even let me *pantomime* to her during Q-time.

I can't help myself. I love to talk! So does Sally, but she is a sneakier whisperer.

P.S. Just for the record, I was *not* one of the kids who almost exploded Tommy Flint. It wasn't that I especially like him that I didn't give him my hot dog. It is because I LOVE hot dogs. Correction! Past tense! I "loved" them. It's hard to believe no more hot dogs EVER.

Thursday, April 27

Dear Journal,

I stood up for my vegetarian rights today and asked, "Mrs. Isner, why don't you offer a vegetarian meal?"

Mrs. Isner has worked in the cafeteria forever, some say 25 years, others say 50, and the rumor is she has never smiled. In my two years of experience, she's kept her record perfect—even when people try to trip her up by telling hilarious jokes about school lunches.

Mrs. Isner put down her ladle and stared at me like I was from outer space. "Vegetarian? Are you one of them? All you have to do is ask," she said.

I was excited because now I wouldn't have to worry about getting caught trading my meatloaf on the black market.

I said, "I need a vegetarian platter then, Ma'am."

She handed me two pieces of bread and a small packet of peanut butter. "Help yourself to the salad bar," she said.

Everyone *knows* you only eat the salad bar when you have early lunch. By the time we get to the cafeteria, the salad bar is repulsive. Unless you want cottage cheese with chocolate pudding swirls, or crushed pineapple with pasta floating in it, you better steer clear.

Friday, April 28

Dear Journal,
    More peanut butter and bread for lunch.
    "Help yourself to the salad bar," Mrs. Isner said.
    I'm sensing a pattern here.

Saturday, April 29

Dear Journal,

    I am not allowed to be a vegetarian anymore. "You're just a kid and can't survive as a vegetarian if you only eat corn, potatoes, and beans!" Mama said.

    I LIKE more vegetables than those, but for the life of me, I could not think of any others when she put me on the spot. Tonight, I found a list of vegetables on the Internet, and I am working on my vegetarian defense so that I will be ready next time. I'll show her I eat more than three vegetables!

Artichokes	Sounds violent!
Asparagus	Looks like long boney green witches' fingers!
Bamboo shoots	Don't they jam these under prisoner of wars' fingernails? Wouldn't they hurt going down the throat?
Beans (Lima, Pinto, Kidney, Snap/Green)	How can all these beans be in the same family? Beans must have their own characteristics and personalities just like Bobby and me. Venola and green beans = good. Bobby and lima beans = evil.
Beets	No, but they are good for pickling eggs! If I held the juice in my mouth, would my teeth turn purple?
Black-eyed peas	Nope. Do the other vegetables beat them up?

Broccoli	I don't THINK so, but I like the way it looks like little trees.
Brussel sprouts	Smells too much like cabbage.
Cabbage	Tastes too much like cabbage.
Carrots	Love them raw! Hate them squishy.
Cauliflower	No way! Looks like brains.
Celery	Crunchy, but only good with peanut butter, and I'm tired of PB.
Chickpeas (garbanzo beans)	Which is it? If a bean, I'd try it. If a pea, no way!
Corn	Yes, in the can! Not on the cob since I tried heating it in the microwave without removing the husk and zapped a worm.

Must sleep. Zzzzzzzzzzzzz.

Okay, maybe Mama has a point. I've only made it through the C's, and I give up. I've never tasted most of these. If I'm serious about being a vegetarian, I guess I should eat a few vegetables. Maybe I could make a list of all the vegetables in the world, and then try a new one every day, or week, or year. Not cabbage. It stinks up the whole house when Mama cooks it.

Sunday, April 30

Dear Journal,

    I announced my plan for eating my way alphabetically through the vegetable world, and Mama raised one eyebrow about three inches higher than the other and asked, "Did you win the lottery?"

    Before I could answer, she said, "Well, it looks like you'll be eating what we eat then."

    Parents!

Monday, May 1

Dear Journal,

    I asked Miss Wilma how her doctor's appointment went, and she just said, "Oh, it could have been worse, I suppose." When I tried to badger her for more details, she said, "No need to worry," and changed the subject by pulling me into the kitchen to make sautéed asparagus. Not as good as our usual brownies, but not bad! I can check asparagus off my list!

Tuesday, May 2

Dear Journal,

I spent my own paper route money on broccoli and chickpeas to add to our salads. Did my parents even seem to notice my contribution? Noooooooooo.

Instead, Mama put dead chicken on my plate—even though I told her, "No, thank you." When I tried to refuse and move my plate, she threatened to tie the chicken leg around my neck if I didn't eat it and plopped it down almost touching my mashed potatoes. Bobby ate the leg when she wasn't looking, so I guess I won't have a new necklace to wear to school tomorrow.

Anyway, she started talking to Dad about digging the baby bed out of the shed and completely forgot about me or my diet.

Wednesday, May 3

Dear Journal,

Mama looked tired tonight, so I volunteered to help make supper. She already had brown beans bubbling in the crock-pot, so I mixed up cornbread and added some Venola pizzazz with a fresh jalapeño. Dad said, "You're becoming a great little cook. Why don't you make the cornbread from now on?" Instead of getting jealous of my cornbread success, Mama nodded in agreement. See? You do *one* good deed, and then you are stuck with a chore forever.

P.S. I called Miss Wilma to see if she wanted to try my creation. She said she was proud of me but didn't think her stomach could handle the spice. I wish she would tell me more about what's going on with her. She used to be up for trying anything. In fact, I've seen her eat a whole bag of Hot Fries without even reaching for her Dr. Pepper. She still jokes, but she looks pale and sits around a lot.

Thursday, May 4

Dear Journal,

Okay, I'll admit it. I kind of backslid. Mama made my absolute favorite dish tonight—lasagna, and she refused to make a separate meatless pan just for me. So I couldn't resist and ate *a little*. She doesn't really use that much meat anyway, and I stacked the hunks of hamburger I found on a napkin, saving them for my cat. However, when I got up to get more water, the family garbage disposal (a.k.a. Bobby) filched Tiger Lily's whole pile!

P.S. At least Mama didn't gloat because I ate her meaty lasagna. She just acted like it was any other day. And before she could figure out that I wasn't eating the hamburger part and complain about me wasting food, the evidence disappeared. Who would ever have thought Bobby could be so helpful?

P.P.S. Since Mama only makes lasagna about once a month, maybe I can build up some vegetarian willpower by the next time. There's always peanut butter!

Friday, May 5

Dear Journal,

I spotted steak thawing for supper, so I asked Sally to invite me to her house. We had grilled cheese and Campbell's soup since her mom was working. Yum! Sally's been helping me out on steak night for as long as I can remember because she knows seeing meat that's still pink in the middle or bloody juices running all over a plate grosses me out. I repay the favor and save Sally when her mother makes liver and onions, tuna casserole, or stuffed peppers. Maybe this is why we are best friends.

P.S. How many days until school is out? Teachers seem crankier than usual. Ahhhhh.

P.P.S. Miss Wilma offered me STORE BOUGHT cookies today. She said it was too hot to bake. It's not *that* hot. Last summer we baked when it was 90 degrees outside. I think there's more to it, but she just called me "Gloom and Doom" when I tried to question her.

Saturday, May 6

Dear Journal,

My sister is absolutely the coolest person on earth. Mama was nagging me at the supper table for not at least trying the pork roast. Mama said, "I should make you sit there until you eat what's on your plate."

Katrina actually spoke up for *me*. She said, "That doesn't seem quite fair. She's not the one who put it there. When you were a kid, wasn't there something you didn't like to eat?"

Mama pointed her finger at Katrina as if she were going to yell at her for butting in, but all of a sudden she said, "Wild game. Deer, bear, squirrel, ground hog—even turkey. It just had a twang to it."

"Did anything your parents say change your mind about it?" Katrina asked, dangerously.

Mama was quiet for a couple of seconds, lost in thought, maybe sitting at her childhood table staring down at a big plate of bear stew.

"Give that pork to your brother," Mama said, while Bobby grinned from ear to ear.

P.S. I told you Katrina gets away with stuff the rest of us can't. But who cares this time!

Sunday, May 7

Dear Journal,

Mama hasn't completely given in, but she says if I am going
to boycott meat, I should pick up some nutrition books from the
library. Why does she always doubt me?

She said, "Being young and a vegetarian just do not go together.
You *need* protein to grow. Maybe I'll take you along to my next
appointment with Dr. Sisler, and we'll see what he says." She just
said this to bully me into giving up. She knows that doctors' offices
give me the creeps.

P.S. Can't she see I'm the tallest person in my class? Maybe I am
over-proteined.

P.P.S. For some reason, me turning into a vegetarian has put me
back on my mother's radar. Maybe it was better being invisible!

P.P.P.S. Why should someone in seventh grade still go to a
pediatrician? Shouldn't there be a separate doctor for teenagers?
After all, I am twelve and a half! It's humiliating to sit between
a crying toddler and a croupy five-year-old, not to mention all the
crabby moms who have stayed up all night with sick babies. (The
last time I went, I thought a mother was going to bite me in the
waiting room because I was clicking my pen while working a really
hard Sudoku puzzle. I have to bring my own materials because Dr.
Sisler's magazines are the worst. *Highlights* is boring, once you've
found the hidden objects and read "Goofus and Gallant.")

P.P.P.P.S. At least Dr. Sisler has stopped offering me balloons,
so I don't have to carry them out through the waiting room anymore.
He quit when I accidentally popped mine while he was writing a
prescription! Hey, I was just trying to make a balloon animal. No
one understands my creative side!

Monday, May 8

Dear Journal,

Instead of waiting on Dr. Sisler, I researched this whole vegetarian thing on my own. I found some awesome websites, like Tryveg.com. Some are just for children and teenage vegetarians. Now I will have ALL the answers when Mama nags me about my nutrition, which she is doing a lot lately.

Well, that is, I *will* have the answers as soon as I read everything! I printed about 100 pages and could have printed a couple hundred more, but Bobby tattled that I was wasting all the paper, and Dad came and yelled, "Are you trying to wear out the printer? Tomorrow you will be on a different kick. Read every page of that before you print another word!" Parents. It would serve him right if I grew up ignorant and was a financial burden until I was 102 or 103.

Anyway, I told Mama (I am not speaking to Dad) about a website that said only people facing starvation or with rare disorders are at risk for protein deficiencies. She said I should put more effort into homework and less into surfing the Internet. Then she said, "I trust Dr. Sisler to know more about this. The Internet is full of perverts and murderers."

I don't think Internet perverts or murderers are trying to kill me slowly by offering poor nutritional advice, but Mama won't listen. Now, I have to tag along to her next checkup. Wonder if I could bribe Dr. Sisler into telling me if I'm having a sister? If not, maybe I can at least hear her heartbeat through the stethoscope.

P.S. I wish I could only hear Bobby through a stethoscope. Isn't it time he grows up and quits tattling?

Tuesday, May 9

Dear Journal,

Boy, did Mama's plan backfire! She thought Dr. Sisler would simply side with her like adults usually do. Guess what! He is a vegetarian, too! He says he ate meat until a few years ago when he had heart trouble and decided to try a healthier diet.

"At first I just cut out red meat," Dr. Sisler said, "but in just a couple of months, I felt so much better that I dropped pork, and then chicken, and then fish. Since becoming a vegan, I've gone down three pants sizes—without much effort, too. The Mrs. and I started for health reasons and thought of it as a form of punishment, or to say the least, an inconvenience to our taste buds, but then we started ordering vegetarian cookbooks and took some online classes. Meals have never been more exciting."

Mama just stared at him with her mouth open. It's a good thing she was sitting down or she might have passed out.

"But what about children?" she asked. "Venola doesn't need to lose an ounce. If she lost three sizes, we'd see right through her."

"Not all vegetarians lose weight. You and I both know, Marie, that I had a few extra pounds to spare." He chuckled and patted a belly way bigger than my mother's.

"But it can't be healthy for young girls," Mama pleaded. "Don't they need the iron and protein and amino acids you can only find in meat?"

"Not necessarily. I have some brochures," and what he said next almost caused me to fall off the exam table laughing. "I'll write down some Internet sites. Are you hooked up? That's where we ordered the cookbooks. It's a wealth of information!"

P.S. I like the way Dr. Sisler says, "Vee-gan." It sounds fancier than vegetarian. Now that I'm one, I better remember how to pronounce it.

P.P.S. Mama was still skeptical and said she was really uncomfortable with the thought of me becoming a malnourished stick. Dr. Sisler says if I am serious, he will work with me. He wants me to keep a healthy food journal, and he will review it "periodically."

This seemed to satisfy Mama. I heard her say, "I suppose it's just her latest phase."

Her comment reminded me of Mr. Facemeir's sock numbering. Why do adults always underestimate our staying power?

P.P.P.S. I had already printed three of Dr. Sisler's sites. Tee hee. I can't wait to tell Dad that I have a prescription to print that stuff now. If Dr. Sisler and I get to be good friends, he might take me on as an apprentice! Calling Dr. Cutright! Maybe he would let me practice giving shots to Bobby and other degenerate tattlers when they come in for checkups.

P.P.P.P.S. The doctor did let me listen to my little SISTER'S heartbeat! I asked how much he would charge to verify the sex of the baby without Mama and Dad knowing.

"Hmmmmm," he said, tapping his chin with his index finger, "I suppose I *could* accidentally leave your mother's file unattended on my desk. How much have you saved delivering papers over the last year?" he asked. He didn't even crack a smile, but Mama did. Even if he were serious, I doubt if I could afford the information. Most of my money from my paper route goes for Ho-Ho's and orange pop.

As we were leaving his office, I wrapped my arm around Mama and tried to talk her into letting me be her Lamaze coach during delivery, but she said, "Your father has done okay the last six times. I think I'll stick with him. We don't want to hurt his feelings, do we?" Then she pushed my bangs up and gave me a big loud mom kiss, with bright red lipstick, on the forehead. I hate when she does that in public. I'm surprised Dr. Sisler didn't offer me a balloon again after Mama's P.D.P.A. That's what Sally calls a Public Display of Parental Affection.

Wednesday, May 10

Dear Journal,

Mama left the disgusting little hunks of ham out when she made potato soup tonight. When I thanked her, she said, "At some point, your friends' parents are going to get tired of feeding you. Sally's mom is probably ready to send us a bill."

P.S. How long do you think Mama has known about Sally's and my meal exchange program?

Thursday, May 11

Dear Journal,

Since talking to Dr. Sisler, I've tried converting my family to vegetarianism. That way Mama wouldn't have to plan special meals just for me. Katrina is all for it, and she said she had some great black bean soup at her friend Cindy's apartment. She's going to get the recipe. Dad and my brothers say they are having no part of it, and my mother wouldn't even comment. What's the big deal? We already have no-meat nights because my parents like to pinch pennies. Mama fixes a lot of beans, cornbread, fried potatoes, vegetable soup, and macaroni. We're just talking about maybe four meals a week when my family turns into bloodthirsty carnivores.

Even though I have shared all kinds of statistics, they aren't budging. When I told Dad that vegetarians live longer, he said, "If I can't have a good steak—or at least a hamburger once in a while, I don't want to live a minute longer. Who wants an extra six years of celery chewing?"

Bobby said, "Yeah! It's our animal instinct to hunt." Then my brothers grunted like cavemen. Please, God, make sure my mother has a girl.

After our experience at the grocery store, I'm more than a bit concerned. This lady, with kids hanging all over her, struck up a conversation with Mama in the produce department today. She asked how many months Mama was and if she is having a boy or a girl.

I think she just asked so that she could tell Mama about her own experience with sonograms. "Don't trust the doctors. Jeffrey here was supposed to be 'Mackenzie Elise'."

I looked down at the little guy who was spinning around like a dog chasing his tail. Mama's eyes followed, too, and her smile slid off her face.

"I was so excited about having a girl," the lady said wistfully, "and at my shower everyone gave me the cutest pink dresses…." Her voice trailed off and she let out a little sigh. "Not that we don't love Jeffrey, but a lot of that stuff was nonreturnable. Two boys later, I'm still waiting to use those little dresses."

I have no idea who the lady was, but when one mother sees another pregnant woman, I'm finding they are instant friends. She even touched MY mother's belly. Mama didn't bat an eye. Ever since Mama's belly started pooching out, the thing has become a hand magnet. How embarrassing!

P.S. If Jeffrey is five, maybe technology has improved, and they can be SURE now. Please God, let it be a girl!

Late Thursday night, May 11

Dear Journal,

Miss Wilma is having breast cancer surgery tomorrow afternoon. She wasn't even going to tell me until it was over! Every time I've tried to bring up her illness over the past few weeks, she's changed the subject.

Then tonight, when I called to tell her about Jeffrey and his poor mother, I was getting ready to hang up, and I said, "I'll see you after school tomorrow." That's when she just casually dropped into the conversation that she was going to be gone for a few days to the hospital! I had to pry and pry for details. When I asked her why she hadn't told me earlier, she said, "FYI, you're a *bit* of a worrywart. I figured it would be easier on all of us to hold off telling you."

I said, "But aren't *you* worried?"

She said, "Oh, I made peace with my maker a long time ago and what will happen, will happen." Doesn't that sound a bit morbid to you? Maybe she is putting on a brave front. Who wouldn't be afraid!

Would she even have told me if she didn't want her paper canceled for the rest of the week? I *would* be offended if I wasn't so worried about her. I don't want to go to school, but Mama said, "Let the doctors handle this part. You can help her once she gets home."

P.S. I do *not* become as overly obsessed with stuff as the world seems to think. However, I have been thinking about a *few* things since I got the call.

1. Would my parents let me take a leave of absence from school to cook and care for Miss Wilma?

2. Would my cooking kill Miss Wilma?

3. If I become Miss Wilma's live in nurse or cook, should I give up my paper route?

4. Who could feed and take care of Tiger for me if I move out? Bobby? Ha!

5. Will Miss Wilma let Tiger move in, too?

6. Would Mr. Facemeir let my cat live in the funeral home?

7. Could we keep Tiger hidden from Mr. Facemeir?

8. Would Tiger be afraid of ghosts if we moved into the funeral home?

9. Are there GHOSTS in the funeral home, and if so, do they hang around Miss Wilma's apartment?

Ahhhhhhhhh. Must try to sleep!

10. How long can a person survive without sleep?

Okay. Okay. Lights out!

Friday afternoon, May 12

Dear Journal,

No word yet on Miss Wilma, even though I flung papers at porches left and right and hurried home to call the hospital. Since Katrina was at work, I had a chance to get on the Internet, and I found a bunch of stuff about breast cancer. In countries where people don't eat meat, breast cancer is almost nonexistent. I won't tell Miss Wilma because she is dealing with the "C" word enough, and I figure it is too late to change her diet now. Even *more* importantly, she has told me to quit pestering her about becoming a vegetarian, or she is going to move and not tell me where. I'm addicted to her brownies, so I've backed off.

Last night on the phone, when I was trying to persuade her, Miss Wilma said, "I am an old woman, and I love red meat. I don't drink, smoke, or take drugs. I don't even swear—well, not much, unless I stub my toe. If a hamburger is my worst vice, then I think I am doing fairly well. So back off, Girlie!"

She says these things like she's yelling at me and like I am making her crazy, but I know she loves me and that I am her favorite person on earth, even though she never comes right out and says it!

She made me repeat THREE times, "I, Venola Mae Cutright, will never ever try to convert dear old Wilma Geraldine Facemeir to vegetarianism again." Then she told me that as soon as she gets out of the hospital, she and I will create the best vegetarian dishes on the face of this earth.

She said, "I'll be darned if I'm going to let old Dr. Sisler or his skinny little pinched-mouth wife out-cook me! I've beaten them in the county fair bake-off for fifty years, so I'm sure we can steal the title for best vegetarian dish, too, if we put our heads together!" Miss Wilma definitely doesn't like to be outdone.

P.S. It makes me feel better having a plan with Miss Wilma for AFTER her surgery.

P.P.S. I think it does her, too!

P.P.P.S. Please, God, let her be okay!

P.P.P.P.S. I wonder why Miss Wilma doesn't like Mrs. Sisler. Do you think they both liked Dr. Sisler when they were younger? Ewwww! Then again, that's what causes the biggest arguments at my school.

Friday evening, May 12

Dear Journal,

Mr. Facemeir says Miss Wilma is resting every time I call the hospital, which hasn't been *all* that many times, but Mama has forbidden me to use the phone anymore. At first, she said no more calls to the hospital, but then she caught on that Sally was calling the hospital and then reporting in.

"You kids need to give that poor woman, *and* her brother, a break," Mama said. "It's bad enough I let you bother her when she's feeling well."

P.S. Would Bobby sit by me in the hospital if I were sick? Ha.Ha. Only if my parents paid him, and then he would stick straws up my nose or shave my head while I was sleeping.

Saturday, May 13

Dear Journal

I caught Katrina eating roast beef and said, "Hey, you promised to be a vegan like me and Dr. Sisler!"

"A *vegan*? Is Dr. Sisler a *vegan*?" Then she started laughing as she watched me make a grilled cheese sandwich with extra cheese and extra butter. "You're not a vegan, you Moron!" she said.

"Yes, I am," I said. "And don't call me a moron again, or I will tell Mama."

"Oh grow up, get a dictionary, and quit being such a whiney little tattletale," she said, still laughing at me, WHICH I HATE. "Do you even know what a vegan is?" she asked.

"First, I'm not a tattletale! That's Bobby's official title, and YES, I know what a vegan is. I'm not stupid. Vegans don't eat meat."

"And???" she asked, as she put the roast beef away.

"And what?"

"You better do some more research because I'm not *exactly* sure, but I don't think vegans eat any animal products. No poultry products like eggs. No dairy products, like milk or yogurt, or CHEESE!" she said and smacked me in the back of the head and motioned toward my double-decker sandwich.

"No DAIRY? No CHEESE? I can't live without grilled cheese sandwiches! Does that mean no butter? No ICE CREAM?" I was panicking. Maybe I wasn't cut out for this vegetarian thing.

"Nobody says you have to be a vegan, Silly! Different people have different beliefs. I believe in cutting back on meat for health, but I like a smidgeon now and again." She licked her beefy fingers. "You, however, don't want to eat it at all. You don't hassle me. I won't hassle you. I don't think Dr. Sisler will be upset if you want some eggs and milk."

I don't like milk, especially plain old white, but Mama lectures me to drink it for calcium. Grownups should learn that trying to force a kid to drink something that is good for her doesn't make it any more appetizing. When Mama starts the Food Police thing, it turns me off more. She SHOULD just make sure there is a LARGE container of Nestle Quik and ice cream in the freezer at all times, which would be a job for Superman with my four piggy brothers. If she could do that, I'd get plenty of calcium without her having to nag. Milkshakes—YUM!!

I started thinking about Dr. Sisler. No ice cream in his freezer EVER? What does he put in the plastic egg holes, and does he put something else in the MEAT and CHEESE bins, or just leave them empty? Is that where he stores his tofu and TVP (textured vegetable protein)? He says he can't tell the difference between meatloaf and TVP loaf. If textured vegetable protein loaf is as squishy and gross as school meatloaf, who cares! Yuck.

"Dr. Sisler didn't say anything to me for having a grilled triple cheese sandwich in my journal, except that it was high in fat," I told Katrina, "so he must not think I'm a total loser."

Katrina took a bite of my sandwich and laughed. "Dr. Sisler isn't a fanatic. He just wants you to be healthy." I couldn't believe Katrina and I were having a grown-up conversation and she had let my "loser" comment go by without seconding that I am the biggest one on earth. She is usually more of a smart-alec, but then again, so am I!

Katrina began to leave the room but turned back around with a big grin on her face. Then she did something I can't ever remember her doing before. She whispered, "How about if you and I tiptoe out of here without the he-man carnivores hearing, and sneak off to Dairy Queen for some REAL dairy products?"

P.S. When Katrina said vegans don't eat eggs, I didn't think that would be a big deal because eggs are one of the most rubbery, slimy

46

foods around, but does a vegan not eat cake with eggs baked in it? Can you make a cake without eggs? Even more important, what's in icing?

P.P.S. I don't think my mother would let me stop drinking milk, even if I wanted to. But no lasagna? No cheese? No milkshakes? Oh boy. How far does this thing go? Does it hurt the cow to be milked? And what happens if I quit drinking it? Will I be hunched over permanently like Grandma? She is just bent over a little with Osteo, but it makes me nervous about my future because she drank lots of milk her whole life, and apparently *still* didn't get enough calcium. It doesn't help that Mama reminds me about Osteo *every* time she sees someone even slightly slouching. She says, "Do you want to be like that?" Sometimes she is determined to scare me into doing things. And she's good at it. Are all mothers?

P.P.P.S. Could Grandma be humped over from quilting and sewing? I'll give that up before I even start.

P.P.P.P.S. Poor Dr. Sisler! Do they make vegan ice cream?

P.P.P.P.P.S. They do! I just found this website for Tofutti and all kinds of ice cream substitutes. They probably taste like glue. I don't know what soy is or where it comes from, but vegetarians even use it in fake ice cream.

P.P.P.P.P.P.S. According to my printouts, vegans don't even eat honey! I never thought about being nice to a bee before!

P.P.P.P.P.P.P.S. Yikes! I better go. Katrina said give her fifteen minutes to get "fixed up" (yuck), and then meet her by the car! I don't want to be left behind!

Way later Saturday, May 13

Dear Journal,

Oops. Katrina and I left the house without telling anyone.
Mostly Katrina is in the hot seat. We never paid any attention to
how late it was when we left, and then she drove around a little,
while we ate our LARGE dipped cones.

Dad and Mama heard Katrina leave, but they didn't think
anything of it because she is allowed. It was when Mama stopped
by my room and noticed my TV was on, but I was missing, that she
started to panic. She never once thought I might be out on the town
with Katrina because like I said earlier, Katrina NEVER EVER
takes me anywhere.

Uh-oh. Katrina just slammed her bedroom door. Is she mad at
me for not leaving a note or mad at my parents for yelling when she
was doing a good deed?

P.S. The Gestapo was too upset with Katrina to scold me for
leaving the TV on and wasting electricity. Yahoo! (Sorry, Katrina!)
For once, I'm going to bed quietly without a bazillion warnings.

Sunday, May 14

Dear Journal,

Miss Wilma is doing well. I talked to the nurses six times and her brother twice in the last day and a half. At first, the nurses wouldn't tell me anything because I'm not a relative, but I called back and pretended to be her granddaughter. Tee hee. I hope if they mention me to Mr. Facemeir, he doesn't rat me out.

I know it is a lie, but I FEEL like her granddaughter, and Miss Wilma will enjoy hearing about me tricking the nurses. Laughing won't cause her stitches to pop, will it?

P.S. My parents gave Katrina pizza money because they are going baby bed shopping. Apparently, I was rough on the old one—a true master of escape, and if anyone breathes on it now, it falls apart.

Mama announced the game plan when Dad got home from work. "What's wrong with the one Venola and the others used?" he asked.

Mama wasn't backing down, and I could tell she had thought all day about her word choice, just like I do when I am finagling. (Where do you think I got my top-notch persuasion skills?)

"The boys took that old thing back to the outbuilding," she said. "It's too wobbly to withstand another Cutright child. We bought that bed *used* when Katrina was born, and if you'll remember, Venola was out of it more than in. It's a wonder Little Houdini is alive as many times as she bumped her head escaping. She always had a goose egg!"

Bobby chimed in with, "So that's what's wrong with her! Brain damage!"

So I HAD to smack him.

Mama wasn't about to let our bickering make her miss a sale at Sears, so she quickly tossed Dad the clincher. "Your child deserves better." She had his clothes laid out on the bed, and the two of them were out the door within five minutes.

That's when World War III started. Six voices, but money enough for only three pizzas. Katrina took charge, as always, and called in two extra-large Mega-Meats for my brothers and a medium Flame for us "vegetarian" girls.

She isn't as serious as I am, but at least SHE is supportive of my new lifestyle. I'm glad we are both doing this vegetarian thing because we don't have much in common, other than I wear her hand-me-downs—which isn't a bad deal, since she has fantastic taste! Katrina is pretty and gets huge tips, which since she loves to shop and sew, translates into a lot of nice used clothes for me! She should quit waitressing and go to a clothing design school. Maybe I will suggest this if she continues being nice. I wish I had her talent! I'm not really good at anything besides annoying my brothers.

P.P.S. My parents are stopping by to see Miss Wilma. They took the three cards I made her. I wanted to go, but they said she needs her rest and that when the two of us are together, we get too rowdy. Who would have thought a teacher and I would be separated for being ornery?

Monday, May 15

Dear Journal,

Too weak to go to school. The Flame kept me up all night. Katrina lives by the motto "the hotter, the better," and since we are bonding lately, I copied her, but even she picked off some peppers. I should have followed her example, but Bobby dared me to eat mine *and hers*. He paid me $2! What could I do?

By bedtime, my lips were on fire and actually peeling. I must have touched my eyes with pepper juice on my hands because my eyes wouldn't stop burning and watering. To calm me down, Katrina put saline solution for her contacts in them, but that was like adding fuel to a fire.

I held a paper towel with ice on my stinging, swollen, throbbing lips and a cold wet washcloth on my forehead, until I went to sleep, but then twenty minutes later I woke up the hard way. My stomach sounded like NASCAR, and Mama sat up with me while I cried. Yes, I *cried* like a baby. I couldn't help it.

At one point, I had a bad cramp and screamed out, "I'm dying! Take me to the emergency room."

"Maybe you can share a room with Miss Wilma," cracked Mama. I don't think it was funny for my mother to laugh when I was at death's door.

Later when I was doubled over, I promised God never to eat hot peppers again, which led to a lecture on gluttony and moderation. Nothing like getting hit over the head with a sledge hammer when you are already suffering!

P.S. Mama and Dad yelled at Katrina for ordering such a thing as a "Flame." At the time, I was glad, but it wasn't really her fault. After all, she did tell me to STOP eating all the peppers.

P.P.S. Can you believe Mama tried to blame my "new-fangled

diet" for my unfortunate illness? She is such a meat pusher!

P.P.P.S. I guess it *was* nice of her to sit up with me, and she didn't mention the baby once. It's just a shame to have to be in pain to get noticed.

Still Monday, May 15th

Dear Journal,

Sally said I didn't miss anything at school. The standardized testing is over for the year, so there isn't much homework. Teachers know that over the summer we will forget any knowledge they stuff into our heads now.

School will be out in one month! I am working on a deal with Bobby to take my paper route, so I can go to camp with Sally, but things aren't final. He drives a hard bargain and wants all the profits and an additional $10 from my savings. Plus, Mama may need help with the baby, depending on when she is born.

P.S. Notice I am insisting on "she"? A sister would *never* use extortion on another sister.

From: "Missy"<coolgirl@belington.com>
To: "Venola"<cutright1@mtnbelle.net>
Date: May 15; Time 22:37
RE: Happy 13!

You are invited on Saturday! Missy's turning 13.
Party starts at 13:13. If you haven't guessed, the
party theme is 13, so if you are looking for the
perfect present(s), keep this number in mind! (Just
kidding. No presents, please.)

P.S. I wanted to have the party on the 13th, but my
parents said I had to wait until my *real* birthday
or I would just whine to have another party on the
20th.

P.P.S. Sorry you are sick. Sally told us about your
unfortunate pepper "incident."

Monday, still later, May 15

Dear Journal,

Ahhhh! Will I ever live down the mortification of everyone at school talking about my digestive tract disaster? Sally obviously can *not* keep a secret. What part of "just between us" sounds like "Please broadcast this to the entire student body"? It's my own fault for forgetting to swear Switchboard Sally to supreme secrecy.

On the bright side, maybe it was Sally's description of my suffering that scored me an invitation to Missy's party!

P.S. Do you think Sally was already invited, and I was a last minute add on? Ugh.

Tuesday, May 16

Dear Journal,

I shouldn't call Mama a "meat pusher" right before I drift off to sleep. I dreamed she was chasing cows with a giant scalpel, and I was trying to protect them, but she had super-human powers. The cows were bawling and stampeding. I was afraid of Mama, but also of the cows stomping me!

Later in the dream, Mama was on a street corner wearing a doctor's lab coat, selling steaks and baby-sized leather jackets that Katrina had helped her make.

"Psst," she said and cracked open her coat. "Can I interest you in one of these thirteen freshly made jackets?" Next thing I knew, she was making me feel guilty for not wanting to wear one.

I said, "But Mama, that baby thing won't fit me."

"Sure it will," she said and seized my arm, tugging and stretching the leather jacket around me like it was a straightjacket. I knew if she got it on me, I'd shrink and be a baby forever, so I ran and ran, but I knew she was behind me, and I started mooing like one of those cows.

P.S. I never really thought about leather before. I've always thought people shouldn't kill animals to make fur coats, and somewhere way back in my mind, I knew what leather was, but I just blinked it away. Maybe this dream is a sign. If I'm a real vegetarian, can I wear my leather coat? Aren't a lot of shoes made out of leather, too? And my purse and my wallet? Yikes! Life is becoming very complicated, and all because Mr. Bookout made me look through a microscope! I hate when he makes me think!

Later Tuesday, May 16

Dear Journal,

Today I was well enough to return to school, which was really important—but not because of the history test. I could have lived without that! But because if I missed another day's school, my parents would never let me go to Missy's exclusive overnight slumber birthday party on Saturday. I'm so tired, but Mr. Bookout really piled on the homework. Who cares about photosynthesis? I wish Miss Wilma was home. She could explain it a lot better than this textbook!

Wednesday, May 17

Dear Journal,

I just found out that Missy only invited *three* people, Karla, Sally, and me. Since I'm the only one invited who isn't a cheerleader, I'm wondering if Sally made her invite me. I asked, but Sally denied it. Why else would Missy invite me only five days before the party? Hasn't she been planning it for months? I would!

What present do you take someone who has everything, especially since it has to have a "13" theme? Sally swears she hasn't found anything yet, and said, "I might just buy a card. The invitation said Missy doesn't even expect a present."

I'm not falling for the "no present routine" for even one minute. Who doesn't want a present? No one's *that* rich. I bet Sally is keeping her present a secret so that it will be better than what I come up with. Sometimes she acts like she'd rather be Missy's best friend instead of mine. I've got to find out what she's getting Missy!!! But how?

It wouldn't matter anyway. Anything I can afford 13 of, Missy probably doesn't want. Pencils? Hair clips? Sheets of paper? Why is Missy inviting me? Most days she doesn't even talk to me.

Oh well, I *am* going because I'm dying to see her house (which is gigantic). I always wondered what her room would look like. So this time Saturday, I'll let you know. I hope this isn't a trap. She is being too nice lately.

P.S. The hospital is keeping Miss Wilma longer than she expected. "They think I have a dollar left, and they want it," she said when I asked her why.

Thursday, May 18

Dear Journal,

Things sure are changing around here! After supper, Mama and I watch *Entertainment Tonight* and catch up with what's happening in the celebrity world. It is usually just the two of us because Dad can't stand the show, and everyone else is busy with part-time jobs. Dad says Mama and I are wasting our brains, but since we outnumber him and won't let him switch to the regular news, he goes outside on the porch and reads the paper or helps the boys mow yards.

Ever since I was a little girl, I've sat in front of Mama while she brushes the tangles out of my hair and braids it, or if I am tired, I lie down on the couch beside her and use her lap as a pillow—except *today*, I was literally kicked out of my favorite position.

"Honey, you're going to *have* to move," Mama said, lifting my head. "The baby's just not allowing this tonight."

I looked up just in time to see her blouse jerk. I watched a movie once where aliens popped out of people's stomachs and took over the world, and the action under Mama's blouse gave me a flashback for a second or two. She took my hand and pressed it across her squirming stomach. What a strange feeling to know that the baby was right inside, feeling the pressure of my hand.

When the baby settled down, I returned to my human lap pillow to finish *Entertainment Tonight*. That's when I felt a jab right to the back of my head. The baby was actually kicking or elbowing me off *my* mother's lap!

"Hey, I was here first!" I said, no longer needing Mama to place my hand where the movement was. The flowers on her blouse were lifting up and down, just like a mole was trying to push his way out of the ground beneath them! "The baby must be a brother as stubborn as it's being."

Mama and I both started laughing, and the movement under her blouse subsided, but before I could lie back down, Mama placed a throw pillow next to her and patted it. "For now, let's give in to his or her demands. There's not much of a lap left for you anyway."

Mama was right. She's definitely said good-bye to her waistline. Yesterday when she drove me to school, her belly rubbed the steering wheel—even though she scooted the seat to where her feet barely touched the pedals. It's a good thing school's almost out because unless her arms grow, before long, she won't be able to drive me on running-late days.

P.S. Isn't it supposed to be *my* turn to boss someone around since my siblings have bossed me around for 12 1/2 years? If this is any indication of things to come with the little dictator, I might as well pack my bags and move in with Miss Wilma.

Thursday, later, May 18

Dear Journal,

I was so bored tonight that I went for a walk with my parents. Since the weather turned warm, they have been strolling around the neighborhood because Dr. Sisler said the baby needs exercise.

I doubt if I go again for many reasons. First, Mama walks like a wind-up toy duck whose batteries are about to give out. Second, my parents have never met a stranger and would talk the bark off a tree. I thought they were taking *long* walks, but it turns out they chitchat with every neighbor about flower gardens, garbage pickup, and every other boring thing you can think of. Third, people in cars give you strange looks when you walk with your parents, like maybe your family is too poor to have a car. However, the absolute worst thing was that the sidewalk wasn't wide enough for three, and Mama and Dad held hands, so I followed behind like a stray dog or walked backwards in front of them, nearly tripping over every tricycle and skateboard in the community. When they put their heads together and whispered, I had to ask them to repeat it, and they only did sometimes.

"It's not polite to whisper," I finally said, pouting.

"It's not polite to listen in on someone else's conversation either," Dad said.

Didn't they want me to go along?

Friday, May 19

Dear Journal,

My life is so dull! I don't even have any homework. Dad is at work, and Mama is taking a nap, which is something new because of the baby.

Sally works at her mother's floral shop, and when I called and offered to help after I finished my paper route, her mother said no.

Even though Sally put her hand over the phone, I heard her mom say, "All you two do is giggle, gossip, and yell out the door to boys. You'll see her tomorrow at the party."

Okay, so she knows us.

So next I called Miss Wilma. I *know* she is in the hospital, but she is sleeping a lot. Doesn't that mess up her nighttime sleep? That's what Mama always tells *me* when I fall asleep on the couch after school.

So with this in mind, I decided to do Miss Wilma a favor and make sure she was awake. Sure enough, she was napping and woke up groggy and grouchy.

"Did you think about what 13 things I should take to Missy's party?" I asked when she answered the phone.

"It's the only thing that's been on my mind for days," she wisecracked. "In fact, I was dreaming about it when you woke me."

"What did you come up with?"

"Don't remember. I had something really good and the phone rang. Maybe if I go back to sleep, it'll come to me."

"No, don't! Just give me one idea."

"Thirteen night crawlers."

"Be serious."

"I am serious. You don't like her."

"I do, too."

"That's not what you are always yammering on and on about to me."

"People can change."

"Okay, then. Thirteen of your favorite books."

"I'm not parting with my books."

Miss Wilma sighed. "Well then make her something, Venola Mae Cutright. Cookies. Cupcakes. Have I taught you nothing?"

"If I get them made, do you want me to bring you one?"

"I think I'm calling it a night soon," she said, yawning. "It's been a full day of poking and prodding at Rip-Me-Off General."

Nobody wants my company.

Friday, later, May 19

Dear Journal,

I am a lousy cook *and* daughter. I followed Miss Wilma's advice and mixed up chocolate cupcake batter. I should have concentrated on just that, but while the second batch was in the oven, I got ahead of myself and started making Miss Wilma's homemade fudge icing. So I was on the phone to her, asking a question and stirring away, when I smelled something burning. You guessed it—the cupcakes. When the smoke detector went off, I bumped my hand against an oven rack and screamed.

This is where the bad daughter part comes in. Mama jumped up from her nap and ran to the kitchen. Now she is dizzy and on the phone to Dr. Sisler. He is stopping by to check her blood pressure. Maybe if I give him one of my super cupcakes, he won't charge for a house call.

P.S. Wonder if he would charge to look at my burn. It hurts.

Friday, even later, May 19

Dear Journal,

Dr. Sisler just stayed a minute. He said, "Marie, lots of women have lower than usual blood pressure during their second and third trimesters. Try not to spring up too fast. Your cardiovascular system is undergoing dramatic changes."

He looked around the kitchen at the stacks of dirty dishes and chocolate-covered mess. "Maybe Venola could help out a little more in the kitchen until after the baby gets here."

That brought color to my mother's pale cheeks. "I'm not sure my kitchen can survive much more of Venola's 'help,'" she said, looking from countertop to countertop as if she were expecting an avalanche of bowls and pans any second.

"I was just starting to wash up my mess when I got burned. Now the hot water hurts my wound," I whined.

Dr. Sisler slapped on some medication and a Band-Aid.

"Rubber gloves should keep your injury nice and dry," he said. "Better get started if you don't want to be late for school on Monday morning."

Ha.Ha. Adults are so funny.

P.S. I didn't even offer him one of my super-duper ooey-gooey cupcakes.

P.P.S. He probably wouldn't have eaten it anyway. After all, they were made with eggs. And he made a comment about sugar not being good for anyone. What *does* he eat???

Saturday, May 20

Dear Journal,

Talk about sabotage! Missy said not to eat before coming because her parents were letting us have a banquet for queens, but she never said it was a meat party! Just think how many animals had to die so that she could be spiteful!

Sally and I walked to Missy's together. I figured we would both be a little nervous about going into the Fowlers' mansion. When I told Missy that I'd never met one college professor, let alone two, she said it was no big deal and her parents would probably just be grading papers all evening and not bug us at all. Still, I was afraid I'd say something stupid when I met them. I practiced what to say: "Good evening, Dr. and Dr. Fowler." Or "Good evening, Drs. Fowler." OR "Good evening, Missy's parents." It is a lot easier when people are plain old Mr. and Mrs.

So anyway, we rang the doorbell and gawked at the sculptures on each side of the door. Sally and I grinned, but before either of us could make a smart-alec remark, a lady in a gray and white uniform opened the door. I'd seen her at the grocery store before and figured she worked as a maid in a hotel. I never thought she could be an individual maid for someone I knew.

She said, "Good evening, Girls. Missy said to show you up to her room. Her parents apologize, but they both are working tonight, so if you need anything, I'm Mrs. Spencer," and she began walking slowly towards an enormous staircase.

At the landing, we took the stairs that curved to the right, and I started praying that I had wiped all the dirt off my shoes because the wooden stairs had a light pink-flowered runner of carpet all the way to the top. I looked back to see if Sally was worried about her shoes, but she was just casually walking without gawking at everything, and then it hit me—it was MY first time. Sally had been here before and neglected to tell me!

I didn't have much time to consider Sally's betrayal. Mrs. Spencer tapped on a door and opened it gently. "Here are your guests, Missy!" she said, like she was talking to a fairytale princess.

Then Mrs. Spencer closed the door behind us, and we were standing in the prettiest room I've ever seen. I've always dreamed of living in Jeannie's bottle on that old sitcom *I Dream of Jeannie*. I love those red velvet-covered couches and matching throw cushions, but if Jeannie had any real powers, she'd blink and trade with Missy in a second. The king-sized bed had a sea-foam green poofy spread, and pale gauzy curtains. Any second, I expected harem girls to carry in baskets of fruit for Missy to sample.

She had a couch with tiny pastel flowers, so loaded down with throw cushions there was barely room to sit, and two sea-foam velvet-like chairs faced the couch like they had been having a cozy conversation before we so rudely walked in and interrupted them. To one side was a white marble fireplace, and when I turned my head, an entertainment center covered a whole wall, displaying a colossal stereo, a flat screen TV, and best of all, a desk built in with rows and rows of beautiful new books above it. Missy doesn't even *like* to read—except for gossip magazines. But then my eyes landed on the prize jewel of the desk—a sea-foam PHONE!

My mouth must have been hanging open because Missy giggled and said, "Oh, Venola, you've never been here. I forgot." I didn't want to give her the satisfaction of knowing I was impressed, but I couldn't help it!

"Wow! You have your own phone?"

"A couple," she said, like it was no big deal, and she pointed to the one on the nightstand. "Actually three, if you count the one in my bathroom. Four, if you count my cell phone."

No kidding, not only does the girl have her own bathroom,

but she has a phone in it. I had to sit down before my legs gave out. Someone (probably not Missy) had spread out four white air-mattresses in front of the TV. I dropped my tattered old sleeping bag on one and plopped down, while staring up at Missy's fancy white ceiling fan.

"You've got it made," I said, and I think this made Missy halfway like me for a minute.

"Oh, you silly girl," she said, and she took Sally by one hand and pulled me up by the other and said, "Come on, let's eat. Karla is going to be late. She's been arguing with Jason all afternoon, and now they are on the phone making up!"

She walked us into what she said used to be her "play room" but was now her computer room, and she spread out her arms like a gameshow girl showing us the prizes we had won. The food was on a table, the size I usually only see at family reunions or at school. All this for the four of us. Talk about a feast! I recognized chicken wings, bacon wrapped around little mushrooms, pepperoni rolls, bite-size corn dogs, crab cakes, shrimp, a tray of cold cuts, dips, and some crackers and cheese. There were a few other fancy-fishy looking things that I didn't quite recognize, but I didn't want to look stupid and ask. That's when it hit me. Yikes, I'm a vegetarian now. So I pulled my hand back from the pepperoni rolls and moved down to load up on cheese and crackers.

I had already put four mini-corn dogs on my plate, so I peeled them and ate the breading slowly. Is it cheating to eat the cornbread? A little of the hot dog juice would soak into it, hunh?

Oh well, I'm trying. I complimented Missy on how great everything tasted. I didn't want to be impolite. Those wieners were beginning to seem the size of logs because I didn't know where to put them. I didn't see a trash can. My first instinct was to put them down the crack in the couch, but I figured they would start stinking in a few days. So when no one was looking, I fed the wieners to Precious, Missy's miniature Pomeranian. I didn't know that some dogs can't eat wieners. Every dog I had ever known wolfed down any meat they could get their paws on, and Precious was no exception. It wasn't until later when Missy stepped in chewed up wiener particles that I knew I'd made a mistake.

When Missy quit jumping around, waving her hands in front of her face, making gagging noises, and screaming, "Oh gross, gross, gross," she called Mrs. Spencer. I apologized the whole time Mrs. Spencer was cleaning it up and offered to help, but she said it wasn't a problem. Her smile looked a little plastered on like she really didn't want to be dealing with dog vomit. Who would? Missy didn't kick me out. When she calmed down, she said the dog was a nuisance and her mom and dad pressured her to get Precious so they wouldn't feel guilty for working so much.

After making Missy's dog throw up, I felt too embarrassed to act snippy about being a vegetarian at a meat party. Maybe Missy didn't even think about it. I'd like to give her the benefit of the doubt. After all, who needs other food when there is cake? And there was a huge birthday cake, half chocolate and half white, but nobody felt much like eating it because the room still smelled like Precious puke.

P.S. Should I take Precious a squeaky toy for almost putting her in the hospital? I am a vegetarian and supposed to be kind to animals instead of nearly killing one. How embarrassing.

P.P.S. If I bought gauzy material and attached it to my ceiling with some thumbtacks or nails, could I rig up fancy curtains that look like Missy's for my bed? Or would the ceiling start leaking on rainy days?

P.P.P.S. I always thought having a maid would be the life, but not anymore. I couldn't get used to having someone clean my room. I'd always be apologizing. "Please forgive me for throwing my dirty socks on the floor." Could I really say, "Please fill Tiger Lily's food bowl and now that I think of it, her litter pan is smelly too." Could I expect someone to pick up individual kernels after I kick over the popcorn bowl that I always forget and put by the bed?

P.P.P.P.S. Maybe I should send poor Mrs. Spencer a card.

P.P.P.P.P.S. Maybe I should send one to Precious!

P.P.P.P.P.P.S. Baking Missy's present was a fantastic idea. She liked them as much as the scrapbooking stickers Sally gave her.

P.P.P.P.P.P.P.S. Did I mention I ate *three* of my own cupcakes? Oink. Oink.

Sunday, May 21

Dear Journal,

When I called the hospital and told Miss Wilma what happened at Missy's party, she said, "Well, maybe you should throw a party and have all veggies!" She was just joking, but I think it would be a great idea, and I don't mean just to get back at Missy. Maybe Missy wasn't trying to starve me when she planned the mega-meat menu. After all, a few months ago, I would have thought I'd died and gone to heaven to be turned loose on that buffet.

If I had a vegetarian party, maybe some of my friends would become vegetarians, too—that is, if I could convince them that it's not just eating bowls of boiled brussel sprouts and turnips all the time. Then maybe they would quit calling me stuff like "Vegola" and "Veggie Breath." Do I go around calling them "Flesh Eaters"?

P.S. Maybe I will become the world's greatest vegetarian chef. That sounds as exciting as my sister becoming a fashion designer!

P.P.S. Miss Wilma may get out of the hospital tomorrow. She has been yelling to go home since she woke up from surgery. My parents said the hospital probably kept her longer because she is so old. Funny, I never think of her as "old" because she has more energy than anybody I know.

Monday, May 22

Dear Journal,

I am glad I gave Missy the benefit of the doubt because she did something unbelievable! I think. At the sleepover, I told them about Miss Wilma, and guess what Missy did?

Miss Wilma just called to let me know she is home and said, "You little sneak! I didn't know you could keep a secret! I received the beautiful roses from you and your three friends. You'll have to thank them for me because my arm is too sore for writing notes!"

Only Missy could afford two dozen roses! Plus, she asked me if I was going to see Miss Wilma after school. I didn't know why she was smiling like a lunatic, but now it all makes sense. Do you think she is starting to like me?

P.S. If Miss Wilma is too sore to write, what about baking brownies? I might have to try making Miss Wilma some instead of waiting for her to do it. She is probably suffering from brownie withdrawal, too.

Monday, later, May 22

Dear Journal,

Humdrum day at school, but my cooking afterwards had enough pizzazz to make up for it. I baked individual pesto pizzas with artichokes and sun-dried tomatoes for the whole family (and Miss Wilma). Yum. Strike one up for Venola the Vegetarian! The boys ate them and even Bobby said they were "decent," but then they asked if they could drive through McDonald's. They mooed all the way to the car. I saw Dad slip them a five to bring back a couple of Quarter Pounders for him, too.

P.S. I didn't burn even one of the pizzas or the brownies I made for dessert.

P.P.S. I may start taking my lunch to school because the cooks aren't very considerate to the vegetarians. Yes, they always have peanut butter and bread, but how many days can I eat that before my mouth sticks completely shut? Hey! Maybe that's what they are hoping for! It's a conspiracy headed by the principal. Or maybe the teachers are paying the cooks!

P.P.P.S. When I delivered Miss Wilma her pesto pizza, she sniffed it and said it didn't smell half bad, but she only nibbled a few bites, which was more than I can say for my poor snubbed brownies. "I'm sorry, Venola, but I haven't been hungry lately." She looked tired so I didn't stay as long as I usually do. I took out her trash, washed her few dishes (it's fun at someone else's house), and told her I needed to do some homework. I wanted to hug her, but I was afraid I would hurt her stitches.

Monday, still later, May 22

Dear Journal,

Katrina is still mad at our parents for yelling about the hot peppers and the Dairy Queen trip. Ever since then, she has been talking about moving out! (Mostly to her friends, but I am an expert eavesdropper.) It would be fantastic if Katrina left. But *how* stupid would that be? For my sister to move because I ate too many hot peppers? The guilt would eat me alive. NOT! Maybe I could have her room!

Tuesday, May 23

Dear Journal,

Memorial Day weekend is extra long, so we are going to the beach! My parents say that once the baby comes, NO ONE will be sleeping very well, let alone vacationing, so they rented a little house not far from the Boardwalk in Ocean City, which is where Mama and Dad spent their honeymoon twenty years ago. Is it strange to take your six children on your second honeymoon?

Our rental house is "Ocean View." So if I can't sleep, maybe I can stick my head out the window and watch the waves crash in.

My parents took Katrina, James, and Philip to Rehoboth when they were little, but since the rest of us came along, our family vacations have been closer to home. Maybe because Mama is terrified of water and afraid somebody would be dumb enough to drown. (After all, she has witnessed me fearlessly diving out of that baby bed, right?)

I asked Dad if the reason we'd never gone to the beach was his fear of losing one of us. Apparently, he didn't take my "losing" as meaning "drowned" because he just smiled and said, "What a bonus if we'd misplaced a couple of you and a dolphin had taken you to raise! Nah, I've learned not to run off and leave any of you. They always find their way home, don't they, Mother?" He reached over and patted Mama's hand, and they had a big guffaw. They sure don't listen to Dr. Phil about building kids' self-esteem. I asked him if it wasn't a bit odd to call his wife "Mother," but he just ignored me and said, "The thing that terrifies me is the stack of bills that go along with a vacation."

Usually we just go camping at Stuart's Park (about 25 miles) or to my aunt's house in Parkersburg (about 80 miles). How can we afford a real vacation now, with a baby on the way? Maybe with my older brothers and sister making their own money, things aren't so tight. Even I have my own money now, with the paper route.

Sally has been bragging about her and her mom's future trip to Florida since Christmas. It is going to cost over $3,000 for just the two of them! My brother Melvin's car didn't cost that much! Maybe Mama decided if Melvin, Bobby, and I are ever going to see an ocean, it better be somewhere closer and CHEAPER. I don't care— Ocean City, here we come!

P.S. We're not going to any amusement parks, but that's okay. I just want to walk and walk and walk on the beach with my feet in the ocean like the people do in advertisements!

P.P.S. I wonder if they have jellyfish there.

P.P.P.S. SHARKS??? I know, I know, I used to talk about learning to scuba dive peacefully with them, but for now, maybe I will walk *next* to the ocean in the sand! I don't want any surprise attacks ruining the vacation. After all, sharks chewing on me might just send Mama into early labor.

Later Tuesday, May 23

Dear Journal,

Can you believe it? Katrina is passing up a chance to go to the beach. She says her boss won't let her off on such short notice, but I heard her telling Cindy that no way on earth was she squeezing into the van for a geeky family vacation. Sometimes she's like a different person when she is talking to her friends.

P.S. If she hadn't been so nice to me lately, I would have squealed big time.

P.P.S. I wish I could talk a couple of brothers into staying home, too, so that I could have the whole back seat of our GEEKY van to myself on our way to our GEEKY rental house on our GEEKY vacation!

Even later Tuesday, May 23

Dear Journal,

I spent all evening researching Ocean City online, until Dad yelled for me to go to bed. I can't wait until we get there!!! I'm begging my parents to let Sally go, too, but they say the van is going to be crowded as is. Dad said, "Maybe I could tie the two of you on top," but when I started to jump up and down, he said he didn't think Mama or the State Police would go for that solution.

Wednesday, May 24

Dear Journal,

When I stopped by Dr. Sisler's office to show him my food journal and to drop off his paper, I couldn't help telling him about my upcoming beach trip. He suggested packing healthy snacks to take along because fast food places don't "cater" to vegetarians.

"I'll eat fries," I told him.

He shook his head. "No. No. No. That just won't do. Variety is the key! Once in a while is okay, but you can't live on fries. You need food that will give you energy, and remember what your mother said about nutrition?" he asked.

I nodded. How could I forget what my mother *said* about nutrition? She said something about nutrition EVERY other minute or so. Although I would never admit it to her, Mama and I *are* a lot a like. Ahhh! We both do have a tendency to keep at something if it doesn't suit us.

"What do you mean by variety?" I asked. All I could think of were Doritos, corn chips, rippled and regular and barbecued potato chips.

He said, "Take different things that are good for you, and your mother won't bug you to munch on hamburgers or chicken nuggets. Impress her with your maturity."

"Like what? Tofu in a baggie? I looked at it in the store, and it is repulsive and squishy. And you better not be talking about that TVP stuff."

Dr. Sisler chuckled. "Well, I bet I could fix both in ways you would love. Then again, they might not be perfect in-the-car foods." He paused and scratched his chin. "How about low-fat blueberry bran muffins, or raw brazil nuts or almonds, raisins, dried apricots, baked tortillas and salsa, soft pretzels, air-popped popcorn? Oh, I could go on all day. What do you think?"

"I think you should come on the trip!" I joked, and I caught the apple he tossed me as I raced out the door with my veggie journal.

Thursday, May 25

Dear Journal,

I did exactly what Dr. Sisler said and spent some of my paper route money on fruits, nuts, and healthy snacks for the trip. Then my kleptomaniac brothers got into my stash and ate half of it!

I was screaming for them to pay me back, when Dad got involved. "In this family, we share. Do we scream when you drink the last of the milk?" Is this man really my father or an impostor? I think my REAL father would KNOW I do not like milk—well, once in a while with chocolate Quik.

Since my brothers wouldn't admit who were the guilty culprits, I planned to grill them all, snack stealers and non-snack stealers alike, but before I could wring out a confession, the doorbell rang, and there was Mrs. Sisler holding a package with MY name on it.

She said, "Dr. Sisler told me about your trip, and we wanted you to have some munchies! I made enough for you to share," she said, and then winked, "if you want to!"

I thanked her, and after I got over the shock, I remembered my manners and asked her in. I have talked to her several times because she is one of my paper route customers, but she is a nervous little lady and doesn't say much, and I think my four giant brothers and my dad standing behind me like vultures made her feel like they were getting ready to tackle her and her package. She said, "Oh no, I couldn't right now. Thanks so much, Dear," and all but ran down the sidewalk.

I could almost hear the taste buds tuning up in my brothers' mouths, but I marched right past and put the box by my suitcase! Let them go drink the last of the milk. Ha. Ha.

Later Thursday, May 25

Dear Journal,

Mama said I should be kind-hearted and share my goodies with the boys. I say, "Let them eat meat."

I may take one of the muffins to Miss Wilma, but she probably wouldn't eat it if she knew who made it. I wonder what that woman ever did to her. They act just like Missy and me! And their feud seems dumb since they're old! Will Missy and I be like them? I hope not!

My parents and I are going to Miss Wilma's for a visit later, since we are leaving for vacation tomorrow. They are hoping a real live visit will last me 'for a four-day weekend because long distance phone calls are expensive, and I have been calling Miss Wilma at least ten times each day.

Later Thursday, May 25

Dear Journal,

Miss Wilma was sitting in the same big recliner as the day I met her, but she looked a lot smaller than she had just last year. Not just skinnier, but shorter somehow. Had she shrunk in the hospital or a little each day over the whole year I'd known her? From where I sat, I couldn't help noticing how thin her hair had gotten. As always, I plopped down on her armrest, even though Mama scolded me to get off.

"Venola, you don't do that at home, and I don't want you taking advantage of Miss Wilma's kindness here."

Miss Wilma was running her hands through my hair—lightly, not fussing and pulling out the tangles like Mama, just petting me the way I do Tiger Lily when she needs reassurance. I guess she had missed me, too—even though she pretended on the phone she was ecstatic not to be chained in the kitchen baking me brownie after brownie.

I have been praying a constant prayer that they got all of the cancer. I can't help thinking, *What if she had been a vegetarian all these years? Would she have been in the hospital at all?* When I asked her last night on the phone, she said, "Ohhh. You can't predict that kind of thing. I might have been hit by the turnip truck on the way to the market."

Miss Wilma tugged me back down to the armchair and out of my scary thoughts. "Venola is fine right here. Close, in case she gets out of hand," she said, pulling me to her for a little hug. That's when I saw the old sparkle in her eyes and knew that I could go on vacation. The strength in her gaze told me she was going to be okay, no matter what chemo or cancer tried to pull.

P.S. When we were leaving, she said, "Come here and give me a hug before you take off to be a beach bunny."

What I didn't know is, with her strong arm, she tucked a 60-minute phone card and a $20 bill in my back pocket. And she calls me a sneak!

Friday, May 26

Dear Journal,

So far vacation has not gone as planned. The radio says Ocean City is having record-breaking temperatures, which Mama didn't count on. That's one of the reasons we are going so early, because extreme heat makes her downright nauseous when she's pregnant. But even with the heat, she still has her sense of humor.

"Venola, I am as hot as your lips after all those peppers." Ha.Ha. Why can't this family ever let something die?

The closer we get to Ocean City, the hotter it is! I don't think the air-conditioner can compete with all the hot air of four brothers. By the time we get there, we may all be melted into greasy people puddles.

P.S. Mama and Dad have been reminiscing about the beach, the Boardwalk, Ocean City crabs, and the little rental house for the last hour and a half. I wish we could blink and be there.

P.P.S. Obviously they didn't use people my brothers' heights when they designed mini-van seats. Knees are poking me from the left and right, and Bobby's are pounding a steady rhythm, right through the backseat into my spine—ON PURPOSE! If I complain, Dad will pull the van over and make Bobby sit next to me, or at least that's what he threatened the last time I tattled, around 15 minutes ago.

Still Friday, May 26

Dear Journal,
    Trip continues. Slowly.
    We are getting on Dad's nerves with our rowdy joking around.
Actually it is fun when we are picking on someone BESIDES me.
We never ever travel as a family anymore. I had forgotten what it is
like!
    Dad is the only one not carrying on. Maybe he is nervous
something will happen to the van, especially with Mama pregnant.
He had to stop and add air to one of the tires (probably because of
all the weight in the van). I bet our family weighs close to 1,300
pounds, even without Katrina's big rear-end. I tried to figure out our
combined weight, but everyone told me to mind my own business
when I asked for exact weights.
    Venola's estimates:
    Dad   220
    Mama   180 +
    James   200
    Philip   200
    Katrina (not here) 135
    Melvin   190
    Bobby   170
    Me   110

    P.S. If anyone sneaks in my journal and gets offended
that I guessed your weight too high, it serves you right for not
participating in my pursuit of scientific knowledge. I was trying to
calculate if the van could haul us, or if we needed to drop Bobby off
at the next rest area.

    P.P.S. I'm sure he *could* walk. He has lots of energy for kicking
the back of my seat!!!

STILL Friday, May 26

Dear Journal,

Dad has complained 14 times about the price of gas. I am now keeping a running tally of his grumbles. At the last place we stopped, he said, "I should have gotten fuel an exit back. It's two cents higher here! I thought he was going to turn us around and drive back five miles to save 30 cents!" I almost offered to pay the difference, but I decided for once I better keep my big mouth shut. Not everyone needs to know that I have an extra $20, thanks to Miss Wilma, and everyone seems to be getting crankier as the temperature goes up.

I'm beginning to understand why we never go on any long family vacations. Not only are my brothers starting to smell bad in the heat, but I have discovered within the last few minutes that my parents do not travel well together. His last comment has caused it to be very icy in the van, even with the air-conditioner not working properly.

When Mama came back from her most recent bathroom break, Dad muttered, "I could have been to the beach an hour ago if we didn't keep taking all of these bathroom breaks."

"Would you like to be the pregnant one for a while? I'll be glad to drive if you want to switch!" she said coldly, and she pulled herself up into the van with a grunt, slammed the door, stretched the seatbelt to its limit, snapped it across her big belly, and is now staring out the passenger's window like she is looking for a better family to defect to. That was almost a half hour ago. Who ever said silence is golden hasn't gone on a trip with my parents!

I am in the backseat minding my own business because sooner or later everyone will need someone to pick on. Let it be Bobby!

P.S. I hope Katrina remembers to feed Tiger Lily and she shuts the door fast enough not to let my baby escape. This is our first vacation apart. Tiger may think I am moving and try to find me. Wouldn't it be weird if she showed up at the beach?

P.P.S. Maybe I should use my phone card at the next stop (I know there will be one soon), and remind Katrina to watch her closely, so that on the way home, we don't find Tiger hitchhiking towards the beach. Poor kitty!

P.P.P.S. Still silent in the front seat. I would like to listen to the radio, but I wouldn't dare ask! I may not be a genius, but I'm not an idiot either!

P.P.P.P.S. How many miles to the beach? I haven't been paying attention to the signs. I would ask if I had NORMAL parents instead of these statues.

P.P.P.P.P.S. Do you think people would cheer up if I shared Mrs. Sisler's homemade granola instead of sneaking out bites just for me?

Still Friday, May 26

Dear Journal,

Surprise! Surprise! With Mama not talking to Dad, there were no more stops, and I have finally seen the ocean! It isn't anything like I thought it would be. It is SO MUCH MORE! I thought the ocean would be like a postcard picture, with a left boundary and a right boundary, but it keeps going and going for as far as my eyes can see! And then there is the salty smell! And the crashing of the waves is overwhelming. I absolutely LOVE, LOVE, LOVE the sound. I was hoping to see a porpoise jump out of the water, but Dad doesn't think that happens this far north. Fooey.

My brothers and I ran for the water before Dad turned off the ignition. We kicked off our shoes and scrambled across the sand, screaming "Ouch! Ouch! Ouch!" The bottoms of my feet are as tough as leather from going barefoot, and I can normally walk on hot pavement and sharp rocks without howling, but this sand is a hundred bazillion times hotter!

Mama came along behind us with a humongus pile of shoes in her arms. She said, "Just like two year olds!" but she was smiling and her eyes were sparkling the whole time.

Dad has his arm around her, and they both have their feet in the water, so maybe they will go back to acting like humans since we are no longer sardined in the van.

P.S. Speaking of sardines, I haven't seen any, but I saw (AND FELT) a gross little crab just now. Yuck. I was digging with my toes and burying my feet in the cool damp sand, when I felt this squiggly tickly feeling. When I finally saw what was crawling on me, I screamed loud enough for my family to have another good laugh. Am I the only one who does stupid things?!

P.P.S. I'm glad I'm a vegetarian if this gross little crab is what my family is talking about eating tonight!

Still Friday, May 26

Dear Journal,

Ugh! We went to a restaurant that specializes in blue crabs. I knew I was definitely not ordering crabs because of course, a.) I am a vegetarian, AND b.) I can still feel that squiggly thing crawling up my foot, AND c.) THE RESTAURANT STINKS!

The restaurant was so packed that I thought we would never even make it inside the double doors. The line looped halfway around the building and out into the parking lot. Mama complained about waiting, but Dad had his heart set on this exact restaurant because his boss said it is THE best.

Since Mama's feet were swollen, Dad offered to get her a lawn chair out of the van. Of course, she refused. She hates to be made over just because she is pregnant, whereas I would milk it for all it was worth. Dad kept trying to strike up little conversations, saying things like, "The food must be really exceptional if people are willing to wait this long." And then a few minutes later, he said, "My goodness, do you smell that bay seasoning when the door swings open? I'm almost slobbering!"

I was beginning to feel sorry for him because everyone was tired of standing in line and not answering him much, but he just kept trying. Not too sorry because the smell was making me queasy. It smelled like a cross between the cafeteria on fish stick day (yuck), the hallway outside the boy's locker room (double yuck), and Dad's and my brother's dirty sock feet after they mow (yuck infinity). But the family out-numbered me when I suggested pizza. "We're almost there. Don't give up hope now," Dad said and put out his hand to mess up my hair, but I was too fast and jumped out of line. I looked towards the front of the restaurant. If I squinted really hard, I could almost make out the people's faces who were at the beginning of the line.

About thirty minutes later, we finally walked in, and my ears hurt because of all the noise and pounding. It sounded like the restaurant was building on an addition (and by the size of the line, which continued to grow like a giant serpent creeping out of the ocean, I figured they better keep hammering). Then the pounding started sounding a little more like when Mama tenderizes liver. When we were taken in to one of the dining rooms, I saw what all the banging was. People had huge sheets of paper spread out on their tables, and some were pouring metal buckets of crabs out on the paper.

Customers were pounding crabs with mallets at almost every table. "Are they still alive?" I yelled.

"No, you dummy! That's how you eat them!" Bobby said. "You have to crack them open. Now put your eyes back in their sockets and quit staring like a tourist," he said and pushed me towards our table.

"We *are* tourists," I said, which I realize wasn't the wittiest comeback in the world, but I was too in shock at the clubbing of innocent crabs to smart him back properly.

The smell was the worst thing I have ever smelled, including Mama's ramp/perfume combination.

Dad and the boys ordered a bucket of crabs, a dozen ears of corn, and fries. Mama ordered a steak, baked potato, and salad.

"In a seafood restaurant?" Dad asked, like he was married to a complete stranger.

"Doctor's orders," she said. "I have to be careful with seafood because contaminants could harm the baby."

The boys looked like they were about to change their orders to steaks, too.

"That's if you eat a steady diet of the stuff, Guys," Dad said, trying to rally the forces.

"True," said Mama, "but it's different with little ones," and patted her stomach, "so to be on the safe side, I'll stick with beef."

I knew it was probably not a good time to bring up mad cow disease, so I just minded my own business and tried to slide in my order of hushpuppies and fries. Mama gave me her meat-pushing glare.

That's when I spotted "Vegetarian Venue" on the menu. I asked if I could order Eggplant Scampi.

"It's $11.95, Venola," she whispered, "and you might not like it!"

I said, "You *said* I need to try new things, and eggplant is supposed to be really nutritional," so she let me.

I'm not sure if I would have liked eggplant better if I had been at a less repugnant table, but I wasn't able to eat very much. While Mama and I were still eating our salads, the waitress brought a huge bucket of crabs and set them in the middle of the table. The seasonings went up my nose and made me sneeze.

Then my brothers each grabbed a crab and a mallet, and began whacking. Melvin's crab flew about two feet off the table and landed on the floor. Bobby hit a little harder, and his supper would have landed on a nonsuspecting diner, if not for the fast-witted waitress who caught it mid-air!

"Let me guess," she said, smiling, "you've never eaten crabs before." She then proceeded to show them the proper procedure for dissecting a crab. Mr. Bookout would have given her an A+ for sure.

James and Philip beamed like they were geniuses because the pretty waitress complimented them on being smart enough to hold on to their poor crabs with one hand and tap with the other. No Einsteins here.

Midway through the waitress's crab operation, I built a fort out of the extra menus to keep from hurling. When she opened the crab, and the green guts poured out on the table, I think it even disgusted my repulsive brothers. She explained it was because these crabs are grass eaters, but who cares! Guts are guts!

By the time she brought the eggplant, my nose was so full of bay seasoning and green guts that my supper tasted like bay seasoning and green guts, too. And the worst part about the eggplant, it was SQUISHY!!! Five hundred times worse than mushrooms. Mama didn't get too upset with me for not eating it all because she thought I was being nice by sharing with everyone. And I ate two ears of their corn, and some of their fries, so it wasn't a total disaster. Sharing with my brothers may be a good thing after all! Tee hee. French fries – eggplant = Venola wins!

P.S. I can't wait to tell Dr. Sisler what I tried, and if he tells me he can fix eggplant a way I would love, I'll know he is a complete nut and not to be trusted.

Saturday, May 27

Dear Journal,

If my mother has her way, I'll go home even paler than when I got here. She keeps slathering me with SPF 300 sunblock, which is about the same as wearing a winter coat. I only hope it scrubs off in the ocean, which is where I have been most of the day!

I wish I had more money with me. Bobby bought the coolest dragon kite, but he won't even let me breathe on it because he says I'll crash it. Melvin, James, and Philip were being jerks about their newly purchased boogie boards, too, until they found a volleyball game with other high school kids. As soon as they saw girls in bikinis playing, Bobby and I inherited the boards for the afternoon.

Why can't I look like THAT in a bathing suit instead of like an upside down mop? My hair doesn't even look stringy mop quality. I was trying to keep my head out of the water to be "camera ready," but a wave caught me by surprise within the first five minutes this morning, and now I have more of a "drowned rat" thing going on.

Okay, here's what I mean by "camera ready." The most adorable guy is walking up and down the beach taking pictures of people. Sure, he charges $5.00 to stick the picture in a plastic souvenir viewfinder, but it's worth it just to see his million-dollar smile. Since he said I looked like a model in the picture, I ordered one for Sally and me!

P.S. Sand isn't as great as it's cracked up to be. It gets EVERYWHERE—even in the bread bag, thanks to my slobby brothers getting in and out of the cooler every ten seconds. Who wants a gritty sandwich? Their big feet keep kicking it on my towel, too, no matter how much I yell. But the worst part is my knees are almost raw from wiping out on the boards. Ouch!

Sunday, May 28

Dear Journal,

Today I was walking on the Boardwalk with Bobby, and I smelled this fantastic greasy fragrance. My nose led me to a stand called "Thrashers." The lines were longer than the seafood restaurant, but the people walking away had these huge cups of my all-time favorite vegetarian treat—FRENCH FRIES!

Bobby and I only had enough money to split one order, but when we got up to the counter, guess what! They didn't have my second all-time favorite vegetable—KETCHUP! So I asked the guy, "What do you mean 'you don't have any ketchup'? Don't you even have one or two packs in the back you can sell me?"

The guy said all I'd have to do is taste one without, and I'd know smothering it in ketchup was a mistake. When he saw my doubt, he said to try a little vinegar if I must. Then he raised his eyebrows as if to ask, "What about it?" and I heard rumbling because we were holding up the line.

Bobby quickly talked me into investing in the fries even without ketchup, which wasn't difficult because I walked about a hundred miles up and down the beach today. I was starving! The fries were the best thing I ever put in my mouth! (They would have been better with ketchup, and I plan to bring some from our own mini-refrigerator tomorrow!)

P.S. As we were walking back down the beach, we passed Caleb, the Camera Guy, and he waved and said, "Hello, Beautiful."

Bobby said, "Wow, he must be really *desperate* to sell pictures," and then before I could clobber him, he took off running through the sand with the last two fries.

P.P.S. Never go into a French fry "partnership" with an older brother. He must have at least six invisible hands and two extra mouths.

P.P.P.S. Did I mention why I am hanging out with Bobby? I got in trouble for wandering off too far down the beach by myself. I can't help that I was hypnotized by the ocean! It wasn't really necessary for my parents to growl like they did because the sun punished me enough. By the time I turned back and realized I was kind of lost, the backs of my legs were already RED and stinging.

Monday, May 29, Memorial Day

Dear Journal,

No fair! We're leaving earlier than I expected today. No more Thrashers fries or Caleb the Camera Guy.

We packed the van last night, all except necessities, so that we could make a quick departure this morning. Dad wanted to leave extra early, so that the drive home wouldn't be quite so uncomfortable, since the air-conditioner was still being temperamental. However, we whined about not getting to see the sunrise, and he gave in. By the time they corralled my four brothers and me into the van, our "15-minute last-look time limit" turned into more like an hour, so Dad is fuming. It's hard to pull your toes out of the surf when you don't know when they will get to sink back in. (Why isn't the bathtub as much fun?)

I told Mama the bonus for being so late coming back to the van is that my feet are extra clean for the ride home! Let's hope the boys took off their tennis shoes for a good soak, too. P.U.!

P.S. I always get Memorial Day and Labor Day mixed up. Mama says Labor Day is not until the first week in September. When I told Mama it would be cool if she went into labor on Labor Day, she said, "That's not even funny. That's almost two weeks past my due date. With a Cutright child, it's likely to happen, but it's going to be labor enough being pregnant all summer."

Oh well, it was just a suggestion and worth a shot. Later.

May 29, Still Memorial Day

Dear Journal,

Too tired to write on the way home. Everyone slept. I think Dad preferred driving with us conked out. Wonder if he put something in our orange juice?

When I asked him, he just went, "Heh, heh, heh!" like a mad scientist. What a weirdo.

P.S. Too bad my sunburn is on the backs of my legs. Not perfect timing for a long car ride.

Even later Memorial Day, May 29

Dear Journal,

Yikes! Home sweet home? Katrina had a party while we were away, and someone broke Mama's favorite lamp. Katrina said TIGER did it, but then Mama found two stains on the carpet, which she suspects are party-related, and Katrina is in their room being grilled.

Uh-oh.

P.S. The sister truce is officially over. Tiger and I are no longer speaking to Katrina. My cat is not a scapegoat! Or would that be a scapecat?

Monday, really late, May 29

Dear Journal,

I have never heard Katrina so upset. When we are in trouble with our parents, we do not yell back. I repeat, we DO NOT yell back—even Katrina. This time she did.

I was trying to listen outside their bedroom door, but I got caught, and my parents turned on me! "I never want to catch you eavesdropping again," my mom said, and then stepped back into the bedroom and slammed the door. But it didn't matter about not being allowed to eavesdrop because before long, the neighbors were even hearing.

Katrina yelled, "I'm almost twenty years old!"

Then my dad said, "As long as you are living under my roof, you will live by my rules."

Apparently, Mama and Dad thought this was the end of the discussion, and Katrina was "dismissed" to her room.

But Venola Mae, private eye, heard Katrina crying and calling one of her friends, and then she stormed out of the house even though it was close to midnight.

Mama and Dad are wondering where she could have gone. Should I tell—which could get me into trouble for eavesdropping? Or should I keep my mouth shut and try to go to sleep? I want to look rested tomorrow when I go into school with my brand new pre-summer tan! I wonder what I should wear to show it off. White seems to look best.

P.S. Am I shallow for thinking about my tan and lack of original wardrobe when my sister is out this late and my parents are worried silly?

P.P.S. Even worse, am I evil for wondering if she moves out, how quickly should I ask for her room? The baby could have my little 7 x 9 cell as a playpen!

P.P.P.S. It doesn't seem quite fair to me that my mother is allowed to spy on me while I'm on the computer, but I can't listen in to a family conversation that could mean a bigger room for me.

Too early Tuesday, May 30

Dear Journal,

With the trip to the beach and all the Katrina excitement, I
didn't have time to think about the science project that was due
TODAY. I had planned to come up with a plan on the long ride to
Ocean City, but all the tension in the van broke my concentration
and I didn't even open my science text.

We all have to give ten- to fifteen-minute oral reports this week
on "anything that interests us in the vast field known as general
science." I think Mr. Bookout is tired of teaching and just wants us
to do his work. Ha. Ha. I passed a confidential note to Sally saying
as much on Thursday, and she accidentally left it under her desk.

In homeroom, I was informed that I get to spend my last week
of school in detention sitting right next to Mr. Bookout. What did I
ever do to him? (I didn't even sign the note, but he must have taken
it to a handwriting analyst over the weekend.)

Obviously none of us worked on reports over Memorial Day
weekend because no one made eye contact when Mr. Bookout
asked for volunteers. "People, I have been reminding you of these
presentations for weeks," he said, his eyes scanning the rows of our
desks for signs of life.

I wasn't surprised when he called on me to be his third
unfortunate guinea pig because he knows I am not shy about talking
in front of the class. In fact, I think some teachers have a tendency
not to call on me because they are afraid I will never shut up.

However, today was a little different—thanks to my total blank
out about the assignment, so I stalled. "Um, Mr. Bookout, I have
a fascinating topic, but I'm having some, um, difficulty finishing
up my research in such a short time frame. Do you think I could
possibly have one or two more days to complete it? Maybe I could
go last if no one else minds." I looked around the room for moral
support. Everyone was staring at the back of the next head in front

of him or her, chanting silently, "Please do not call on me. Please do not call on me," and one or two brave souls were doodling on their notebooks or tennis shoes.

Mr. Bookout's eyes narrowed, and he tapped out a forbidding rhythm with his red pen on his grade book. "So you are telling me that even with as little as a one-day extension you could be *that* much more prepared to wow us with your report?"

I nodded my head, knowing what was coming next, and the wheels inside my brain were spinning even faster as to what I could possibly answer. I didn't misjudge Mr. Bookout for a second.

He smiled and asked, "Could you at least entice us with your topic and a few preliminary tidbits so as to make the entire seventh grade class dash to general science class tomorrow?" He thought he had me, but his torturous grandstanding gave me time to form a response.

"Yes, sir. My report will be about the benefits of living a vegetarian lifestyle, not only for saving animals from untimely deaths, but also for promoting healthier, longer lives for ourselves." Then I completely bamboozled Mr. Bookout with my knowledge of alternative sources of calcium and protein, information about the free-range myth, and tasty recipes and substitutes like Tofutti.

"It's like ice cream—only it's made with soy instead of cow's milk. Supposedly it's as good as DQ, but the Hi/Lo Store doesn't carry it and says they don't expect to be stocking it any time soon."

Everyone was ewwwing over Tofutti, so I turned to Tommy Flint for support. "There is even a healthier choice for hot dogs, so that you could win your title, and live to see the age of 20 without coronary failure." Tommy looked at me like I was crazy. "There's a fake hot dog made out of wheat gluten and soy protein. It looks almost the—"

I couldn't believe how green Tommy was turning. This was the guy who picked up dead things at the bus stop and chased us around threatening to throw them on us. I was grossing out the captain of the football team with a little soy talk? I hoped I hadn't caused the backs of *his* knees to start sweating like mine had during the squirmy hamburger under the microscope lesson. I decided to try and calm him down before he passed out.

"No seriously, Tommy. The stuff isn't any worse than what's in those hot dogs that you eat at lunch. I mean seaweed is good for you," I said.

Everyone was fake gagging.

Mr. Bookout was standing in the front of the room with his mouth open. I'm not sure if he was spellbound with my knowledge and control of the classroom, or just completely dumbfounded that I hadn't been pulling his leg about the report. I think what clinched his belief in me was when I explained about the different kinds of vegetarians—the lactos, the ovos, even the fruitarians—and I told the class that I had been working with a local vegan doctor on much of my research, and even keeping a journal.

"Venola, you seem more than ready to give your report." He looked at his watch. I'm pretty sure he was calculating that there were still 20 minutes left, and he had figured out that no one else in the class was even remotely prepared to go ahead with a report today. "Wouldn't you like to finish your report now, and then you won't have to be nervous all night thinking about it?"

I begged off and tried to buy some extra time by saying that I had been having trouble finding "textured vegetable protein" at the local grocery to make vegetarian sloppy joes for the class, and had special ordered the stuff, but that it was looking more and more likely that it wouldn't be here by the end of school. (Some students actually had the nerve to applaud about this, so I turned around and gave them a dirty look.) "TVP is supposed to be just as good as hamburger, and Mrs. Simmons is working really hard to get it in for us, so you could be a little more appreciative," I said, completely offended and almost forgetting that every word was a lie and my nose was probably growing with each minute I went on.

I was counting on Mr. Bookout being too tired with the end of the year stuff to confirm my statements with Mrs. Simmons at the Hi/Lo Store. In fact, I started to wonder if a teacher could lower a grade once it's on your report card, just in case they bumped into each other over the summer.

"Well, I sure do appreciate all the effort," Mr. Bookout was saying, "but since you don't think it will arrive before Friday, wouldn't you like to go ahead today?"

Mr. Bookout was just like a Rottweiler hanging on to a hambone! I guess he hadn't come to school with a backup teaching plan in case we all proved to be the good for nothing students we turned out to be.

I wasn't expecting him to push it this far and call my bluff, but I am a pretty fast thinker. "I could, I suppose," I stalled, "but my mother has gone to a lot of trouble and is probably at the grocery store right now getting some supplies for me to use as my Plan B visual aid for tomorrow. I'd really like to have a hands-on component to add to my hours of research, and I could have had it today, but we just got back from the beach late last night, and the Hi/Lo Store was already--"

He put his hand up for me to stop and actually smiled. When I'd started with all the excuses and doubletalk, he had looked a little doubtful. But the more I talked, the more he started to get excited about the genuine learning possibilities for everyone when I give my oral report, or maybe he was just excited about how much time I would more than likely be taking up with the magnitude of my actual report, especially if I could ramble on this long with just my summary and no visuals or handouts.

The two classmates who had stumbled through their reports before me had taken no longer than seven minutes COMBINED—including the time it took Mr. Bookout to coax them out of their seats and up in front of the class to the podium.

First, Karla moped to the front of the room, visibly having a real snit because she didn't know why she should have to go first. Once in front of the podium, she looked at her audience and became a mime. She pretty much whispered inaudibly that her report was on animal testing for purposes of wearing makeup, or at least that's what I put together from the word or two I was actually able to make out. Even though it was a good subject, and I wish I'd thought of it, she didn't have much information, and just repeated that she thought animal testing was bad in about three different ways. Now that I think of it, perhaps she made up her subject on the way to the podium.

Her visual aid was pretty good though. She reached in her purse and pulled out some makeup. Then she showed us which brand of mascara didn't clump and demonstrated by applying it without a mirror. She didn't poke her eye or anything! Then she sat back down before Mr. Bookout could even formulate a question to ask about her report.

By the time Karla had slumped back down in her seat and moved on to applying blush, Mr. Bookout composed himself and said, "So are we to understand from the voluminous research you demonstrated here today that your brand of mascara is a brand that we can trust not to resort to animal testing?"

Karla looked at him like he had just landed from Neptune and shrugged her shoulders.

"Well, with that under-endorsement, I don't think I'll be running out and buying myself any mascara for Friday's big end of the year dance. I suppose my wife will be relieved to know that," he said.

I cracked up at Mr. Bookout's comment. Third laugh all year. Wooohooo. Hey, you have to give him a little credit for trying to be funny, even if he does fail 99% of the time.

After glaring at Karla one last time, he shook his head sadly and marked something in the grade book. Then, Mr. Bookout pretended like he was playing pin the tail on the donkey and lowered his pen to his grade book again, landing on an unlucky draftee. When he opened his eyes, he "volunteered" Tommy Flint to go next. Tommy tossed his NASCAR magazine that he wasn't even trying to hide under his desk and lumbered to the front of the room. He leaned against the podium like he hadn't slept all weekend and couldn't possibly hold his massive body up straight for another minute. He sighed loud enough to lose at least 5 points for lack of enthusiasm, and then told the top of the podium that he had done his research on what else, but the nutritional content of a hot dog. Now this *could* have been a really cool but gross topic, but mostly his information was taken from the label of an Oscar Meyer wrapper that he pulled out of his pocket. After painfully stammering through a long list of un-pronounceable ingredients, he tossed the wrapper about three feet into an awaiting trash can.

"Three points!" someone yelled from the back of the room.

For some reason this encouragement from his peers or the feat itself seemed to give him confidence, and whether it was premeditated or not, he went off on a tangent about the world champion hot dog eating contest, and his new hero, a guy who had eaten over 50 hot dogs in 12 minutes. The more wound up he got, the louder he became. He went from talking directly to the podium to screaming out his finale, which I must admit was quite effective in getting our attention, even during the last week of school.

He yelled, "The teachers say they want us to achieve our goals. I am walking proof that they are trying to keep me from my hot dog-eating championship destiny!"

Everyone was applauding, so he put his fists up in the air like Rocky Balboa and started jogging in place while screaming, "I could have taken the title! Down with the administration!" He sounded like those nutso wrestlers on TV that challenge the Heavyweight Champion to grudge matches.

As wild as Tommy was getting, I thought Mr. Bookout was going to have to drag him forcibly back to his seat, but instead Mr. Bookout merely promised to save Tommy his hot dog at lunch the next time they are served. Mr. Bookout should have gone into politics. He is one smooth operator.

P.S. If I were Tommy, I would have at least tried to salvage my report a *little*. He could have tied the ingredients of hot dogs to the rest of his rampage. In his conclusion, he could have said something like, "And the final two ingredients in hot dogs are a dash of determination and a smidgen of dreams, which is what I will need if I plan to take over the national hot dog eating title." Then he could have walked back to his desk humming the "Wish I Were an Oscar Meyer Wiener" song. That song is very catchy and sticks in your head, so the rest of the class might have joined in, too. The song alone would have scored him a few extra points in showmanship.

P.P.S. Maybe I could become a general science oral report

consultant. I wonder if Mr. Bookout would recognize my style? If I get good, perhaps I could write speeches for famous people. From what I've seen on *Entertainment Tonight*, some of those stars could use help.

P.P.P.S. Was it wrong of me to ask Mr. Bookout to reconsider my lunchtime detention? I was the last one to leave on purpose, and I just casually said, "Since it *is* the last week of school, AND if I do a really, really good job tomorrow, would you consider lifting all or even part of my lunchtime lockup?"

He didn't say, "We'll see" with his mouth, but I saw a glimmer of it in his eyes, and the corner of his mouth did turn up a bit, even though he just pointed to the door and said, "Move it along, Malibu Cutright."

P.P.P.P.S. EVERYONE said my tan looked great, even though Mama did do her best to keep me ghost-colored!

Still Tuesday, May 30, unfortunately

Dear Journal,

I got off the bus in town and spent most of my secret $20 that I carry in the bottom of my shoe for emergencies on almonds ($4.99), baby spinach leaves ($2.08), orange juice fortified with calcium and vitamin D ($2.50), and tiny paper cups ($1.19). Ouch! Good grades are expensive. Oh well, I backed myself into a corner in science class, so I had to pay for my lie—literally.

At first, I thought Mrs. Simmons was going to give me the stuff instead of touch my germ-infested money. While standing in line to pay, I *tried* to remove the $20 from my tennis shoe as inconspicuously as possible. However, Mrs. Simmons must be used to watching for odd or sneaky behavior, so she leaned over the counter to make sure I wasn't trying to shove a bottle of ketchup up my pants leg or a Freezie Pop in my shoe.

Once she saw me straightening out the $20 that had wedged up in the toe region, you would think the proper thing to say would be, "Oh, Venola dear, sorry to mistake you for a scum-of-the-earth shoplifter. What a unique place to keep your currency." But instead, her eyes got as big as a hoot owl's, and when I attempted to give it to her, she jerked her hands back like I was getting ready to burn both of her palms with a hot poker.

Okay, so the money was a little damp, I'll admit that, but I do wash my feet and shoes occasionally unlike some of my brothers.

P.S. I guess I have to find a new secret emergency stash hiding place since Mrs. Simmons infiltrated my security. If she doesn't trust me, I'm not trusting her!

Still Tuesday, May 30

Dear Journal,

Things are quiet on the home front. Apparently, Katrina and my parents have come to a truce. She is staying with her friend Cindy for a couple of weeks, and if that living arrangement works out, and she thinks she can swing half the rent in addition to her car payment, she's moving for good. Hooray!

I tried to find the perfect time to slip in dibs on her room, but things were still too tense over supper to broach the subject. I don't want to wait *too* long because you never know what devious plot one of my brothers is working on.

It's hard to balance the appearance of compassion for my sister and my Donald Trump Go-getter mentality so as not to get in trouble with my overly-sensitive folks.

P.S. Katrina won't be spending much money on new clothes and sewing material now. So my wardrobe will suffer without her hand-me-downs. Plus, she won't be bringing home leftover pizza. Yikes. I just can't win.

Wednesday, May 31

Dear Journal,

Free at last! Free at last! Mr. Bookout was blown away by my 37-minute report, and I no longer have detention. Woohoo!

I tried not to bore my classmates with too many statistics, because kids and teachers both know that we have already checked out and quit learning since the first warm day of spring.

Instead of statistics, I gave the class plenty of human interest stories about chickens. Most chickens have never seen the light of day or felt a fresh outdoor breeze blow through their little feathers. They are forced to live crowded together tighter than we are on bus #23. You know, the kind of stuff they put on the news when they can't find a soccer dad out of control or a celebrity breakup. The class ate it up, and I might have converted a few new vegetarians. In fact, Karla had to leave the room to fix her mascara about halfway through my report.

I think I even had the back row's attention for a few minutes, which is near to impossible because they are only interested in ink-tattooing their arms, books, jeans, shoes, and each other. Every one of them looked up when I told about how some feedlots fatten cattle on grain and "filler" made of disgusting things, such as sawdust and chicken manure.

One of my visual aids was a close-up picture of a pretty little brown calf with big cartoon-like eyes. I had taken the photo just days before when Sally and I were riding bikes on the rail trail.

"Hey," Sammy said. "I ride past that farm all the time, and that little one's always by the fence like he's waiting for me."

"Not anymore," I said quietly, truly sorry to be the one to break it to Sammy. "I asked the farmer's wife what happened to him, and she said since he was a boy calf, her husband probably sold him to a beef or veal farm to be fattened up for slaughter. She said they only keep female calves, who join their mamas on the family's dairy line."

Mr. Bookout was looking like he might start to boohoo. "Okay," he said, clearing his throat. "Now that you have our attention with the humanitarian reasons why we should become vegetarians, didn't you want to mention some basic nutritional information?"

I gave him a small nod, and just like Vanna from *Wheel of Fortune*, Mr. Bookout raised the big scientific charts, which revealed my gorgeous neon yellow posterboard chart that I'd taped up before class. On it, I had drawn a cow with lines out to different dairy products, such as cheese, milk, and ice cream. In rainbow markers, I'd colored in what percentage of calcium the human body absorbs from each.

Next, I passed out my Hi/Lo purchases. Each person received a couple of almonds, a spinach leaf, and a thimble-sized paper cup of orange juice.

"I want you to eat or drink the one that you think has calcium," I announced.

Everyone was whispering and struggling to get the right answer on my mini-quiz. All except Tommy, who was stealing nuts off every desk in a four-foot radius when students turned their heads to talk to the people next to them.

Mr. Bookout's left eyebrow was going up like he thought I might be losing my audience.

"Stop!" I yelled to the class, waving my arms to get their attention. "It was a trick question. They all have calcium," and then I went on to impress them with exactly how much.

Mr. Bookout had a weird "proud dad" smile on his face and was shaking his head up and down in support.

"What about protein?" he asked. "Would we get enough protein for our 'active' lifestyles if we gave up meat?" He put his fingers up in fake quotation marks around the word "active" because he is always fighting the uphill battle to get us up off our couches and away from our TVs and video games to exercise more.

"I haven't eaten meat since April, and I've got more energy than ever," I said, maybe bragging just a little. "Beans, nuts, and brown rice are healthier choices. Plus, I talked yesterday about all of the substitutes for bacon, hot dogs, and burgers that are available."

Before I could move on to my conclusion, Mr. Bookout STARTED APPLAUDING and motioning for the rest of the class to join in.

He asked if anyone had any questions, but there weren't any really hard ones. After all, I had been fending off the Mama-nator for two months.

One guy asked the usual stuff about man's right to hunt since we are the most intelligent animals. And of course Missy had to try to stump me. She said, "Where in the world do we draw the line? Should we not harm bacteria or plants? Those are living things, too!"

I could have given her a really nasty answer in the same tone she asked her question, but I remembered the mystery flowers Miss Wilma received and toned down my reply. I looked her in the eye, smiled, and said, "We all have to make a personal decision about what is right for ourselves *and* what we want on our individual consciences." I never have been able to say "consciences," and this time was no exception. My face started to turn red, and I said, "Oh you know what I mean! We have to figure out what we can live with morally!"

Mr. Bookout looked at his watch and said, "One last question?"

Wouldn't you know it would be a doozy. Tommy raised his hand and before he was ever even called on, yelled out, "What are you going to do with the rest of those nuts?"

if their lives depended on it. The Great Dandelion Battle, as the day will ultimately go down in history, was more serious than any game of kill ball we'd played all year.

That is, at least it WAS before Mr. Bookout and Mrs. Montgomery broke it up, lined us up *eight* minutes early, seated us in the cafeteria, and gave us a lecture that lasted way into music class.

The principal joined our captors, and the three of them glared from one yellow-streaked, mud- and grass-stained, sweaty student to the next.

He said, "This is the group that I am supposed to call my upper class next year? You are acting more like kindergartners! Are you proud of yourselves?" Out of the corner of my eye, I saw Tommy and Sammy elbowing each other and smiling. Apparently, they were.

"I suggest that you take a good hard look at yourselves in the mirrors while you are washing up. You might not like who you see there."

His speech would probably have gotten us completely out of music class, but Karla started swelling up like that girl in the Willy Wonka movie and had to be taken to the school nurse. Several others were sneezing and had runny noses and watery eyes, so the principal stopped screaming and sent us all to the restrooms to get cleaned up. Who would have thought dandelions could cause such an allergic reaction or be so much fun?

P.S. Thank goodness the principal's daughter goes to our school and likes to dance! Tee hee.

Friday, later, June 2

Dear Journal,

Sally, Missy, and I are going to the dance together, and we're all wearing capris. We've decided that seventh grade boys are immature. It was supposed to be the four of us girls, but after the dandelion attack, Karla and her on-again off-again ex had a big huggy-kissy reunion.

We were standing at the bus stop reminiscing about the battle, and Jason said to Karla, "Seeing you so sick made me realize what my life would be like without you in it forever."

Geez, I didn't realize it was such a Near Death Experience. If I get a chance at the dance, I'll have to ask her if she saw any dead relatives while she was walking towards the light and before she was pulled back to earth by the school nurse.

P.S. Wonder if Hallmark makes a card for "Sorry, you swelled up like a big red splotchy balloon during recess"? Maybe Missy, Sally, and I could go thirdsies on one.

P.P.S. Missy and Sally just IM'd me. They think we should wear dandelion chains in our hair to the dance. Surely they are joking because it would equal detention on Monday morning. I'd probably be the only one to go through with it. Maybe a single dandelion behind my ear would be less noticeable? Are my ears too big to wear my hair that way?

P.P.P.S. Can they transfer detention into a new school year? After all, we get out at lunch time on Monday!

Saturday, June 3

Dear Journal,

Got home too late from the dance to write. Not much exciting happened. I guess everyone was either worn out from the school year *or* the Great Dandelion Battle to cause too much of an upheaval. Plus, the principal had teachers and chaperones strategically placed every few feet all over the gym and at each door, so it was hard to find enough unsupervised space to even plan any end-of-the-year mischief.

I guess the warden wasn't taking any chances after the recess incident. He spent the evening swooping in wherever boisterous groups chose to congregate, waggling his bony finger, warning, "Now no monkey business." Whatever that meant!

He did inspire a hilarious new dance that worked equally well for country, rock, and rap. Everyone screeched and scratched their armpits. The guys added a new move where they pretended to pick fleas off each other and eat them, but that part was pretty gross if you ask me. I doubt any of them will have careers as choreographers.

Missy, Sally, and I tried to leave Alcatraz for some fresh air because it was about 250 degrees and we had been bouncing up and down like apes for an hour straight, but we were barred by a couple of no-nonsense moms. Missy used her sweetest honor-roll student voice to no avail. "You can trust us," she said fluttering her eyelashes and flashing a perfect smile. "We'll just stand right out there where you can see us," but nothing worked.

"Once you leave, no re-entrance" was their only mantra. Maybe they were robots wired by Mr. No Monkey Business himself.

Other than the Monkey Dance, mostly our whole class just stood around listening to the lamo deejay music, retelling school events that we already knew, and scarfing down enough coconut-chocolate chip cookies to give Tommy Flint a run for any future food-eating titles.

For this, I spent two weeks going through my closet obsessing about what to wear and $35 of my hard-earned paper route money at Wal-Mart? Nobody even noticed our brand new color-coordinated capris and crop tops.

I take that back. Sammy Potter said I looked nice. Well, technically, he said, "You all," but that still counts, doesn't it? Here's the weirdest thing that happened all evening—he said, "It's kind of cool you're a vegetarian, but meatloaf day isn't as much fun without you." So this is my question, Journal. Does he miss me or my meatloaf? Ahhh!

Sunday, June 4

Dear Journal,

My prayers have been answered. Apparently at Mama's last appointment, Dr. Sisler recommended another ultrasound, and my parents have decided to find out whether they are having a boy or girl. Not sure why the change of heart. Maybe because now that Katrina has moved out, we are painting the smaller room for the baby. That way they will have a clue about which color paint to choose at Lowe's.

Mama almost didn't let me have the bigger room because Katrina's old room is within earshot of theirs and she wants to be sure to hear if the baby cries. This baby isn't even here yet and is already being shown favoritism.

Oh well, with a little finagling and the right present, I scored the larger space. All it cost me was a baby monitor and a hand-written gift certificate promising to help out with the baby during the night.

"I'm going to hold you to it," she said and hugged me. "We can finally put your eavesdropping skills to use."

I don't care if Mama did get the last word. I got the bigger room. Plus, I *am* a night owl and might as well get to know my baby sister while everyone else is snoozing!

Monday, June 5

Dear Journal,
   You aren't going to believe what my friends did! They knew I
was completely bummed about having to cancel Mama's shower.
   So today at lunch, my friends surprised me with a picture book
party in the library. Mrs. Shuman, the librarian, sponsored it so we
wouldn't get in trouble for an unauthorized large group gathering.
Miss Wilma sent a cake, but her card said that she wasn't up to a
middle-school bash just yet. (I guess when you are taking chemo you
have to be careful with germs.)
   Lots of people in my seventh grade class brought in their
favorite picture books for the baby, so Mrs. Davis had to cut the
cake in tiny 1" x 1" pieces, which if you've ever eaten anything of
Miss Wilma's, you know is just not a big enough piece.
   Probably the funniest book was from our cook, Mrs. Isner. She
brought in *Peanut Butter and Worms*. It even came with gummy
worms that you push through the holes in the book. She smiled for
the SECOND time in 25 years when I opened that one.

P.S. You don't think she was trying to tell me something about
the cafeteria peanut butter, do you?

P.P.S. Does a book party count as a baby shower, and if so, can my
mom legally ground me until I am 50?

P.P.P.S. Speaking of 50, there must be at least that many picture
books. The bell rang before I had time to open and count everyone's. I
guess I'll be writing a lot of thank you notes this summer!

P.P.P.P.S. Mrs. Isner volunteered to drop the books off at the
house since I couldn't take them all on the bus. It turns out that

she's not as old as she looks. She and Mama went to school together. She thinks that she can smooth things over about the impromptu shower so that I'll only be grounded until I'm 45. Ha.Ha.

Tuesday, June 6

Dear Journal

Missy, Karla, Sally, and I celebrated our first day of freedom by packing a picnic and biking on the rail trail. I'm sorry for the train conductors and engineers who are out of work, but I am sure glad they turned the abandoned "rails" into a bike trail!

Thank goodness we had extra Oreos and Dr. Pepper and water because we ran into Sammy, Tommy, and Jason on the trail, and they spent most of the day with us.

When we passed the dairy farm, Sammy and I showed the others where the calf in the picture had lived. While we were resting and eating the last of the Oreos, some of the cows came over to check us out. Others moved away like we were going to try and ride them. (I guess cows come in all varieties—nosey, adventurous, distrustful, and shy—just like people.)

In fact, some of these cows reminded us of famous people and our teachers. A beautiful tan one had big lips, expressive brown eyes, and a long, skinny face.

"She looks just like Angelina Jolie," Missy said.

I agreed even though she looked more like Paula Abdul. Missy and I are getting along for the time being, and there wasn't any sense in starting a battle over a cow-look-alike contest.

One suspicious cow walked up and sniffed our breath like we had been eating ramps.

"Mrs. Montgomery?" Sally asked, and we all cracked up.

Another had two white spots around its eyes and looked like it was wearing big thick glasses. It was watching us the way Mr. Bookout does when he thinks someone is cheating.

Apparently, Tommy saw the resemblance, too. He said, "Let's go before that one makes me do an oral report."

P.S. Karla and Jason didn't play the cow-look-alike game. They were too busy staring at each other with their own great big lovesick cow eyes. I bet Karla tipped him off that we girls were going biking! Rat! But if so, she should have packed more sandwiches!

P.P.S. I asked Bobby to deliver my papers because my legs were too rubbery from the bike ride. He asked for $10.00!

"I'll crawl first," I said and wobbled out of the room as fast as my noodley legs would let me.

I would have done it for him for free—or for $5.00 at the most.

P.P.P.S. Mama and I were driving home from delivering papers, eating double-dipped chocolate ice cream cones, which I paid for as a way of thanks. Mama said, "Next time, pace yourself and don't go so far until you build up some endurance. Gas is too expensive for me to drive you every day—even though the air-conditioner feels great."

Maybe she does love me even if she won't be my human pillow.

Wednesday, June 7

Dear Journal,

Oh the agony! During the night, I woke up in excruciating pain like a gorilla was grabbing the back of my calf and twisting. It only took Mama two screams and three "Ow, ow, ows" to make it to my room. And she was worried she wouldn't *hear* the baby!

"Wiggle your toes," she hollered, trying to do it for me. "It's just a Charley horse."

"I can't! It hurts!" I screamed, while wiggling and rocking back and forth on the bed like I needed an exorcism more than a muscle relaxant.

After the gorilla finally let go, Mama had me drink a glass of water and told me to go back to sleep, which I did once I was sure the invisible gorilla wasn't going to sneak back in and pinch my leg again.

But this morning, I felt like I had a whole gorilla family sitting on top of my legs. Mama said, "Walk it off," like she used to be an Olympic coach or something. Now she's sent me to ride a few laps around the neighborhood.

When I complained that my legs hurt too bad for bike riding, she said, "Cleaning the bathroom would probably help those muscles stretch out, too." I grabbed my helmet and disappeared out the door. If I'm going to be in pain, I might as well have fresh air and sunshine.

Ugh. She's just spotted me sitting under this tree writing, and she's pecking on the window. Shouldn't she have her feet up resting instead of spying on achy old me? She should start her own boot camp.

P.S. I wonder if Sally is as sore as I am, and if she will admit it. I would have emailed her this morning to check, but the computer is all the way down the hall in the living room, and I didn't feel like hobbling that far.

Thursday, June 8

Dear Journal,

I went with Mama to her appointment even though Dr. Sisler said that he doesn't need to look at my vegetarian journal anymore.

At first, I was afraid one of the rugrats in his office would have something contagious, like the measles or a runny nose and ruin my summer vacation, but I braved the waiting room on the off chance that I might get to see the ultrasound, WHICH I DID!

Dr. Sisler took his time explaining about how the baby can open its eyes now, which is pretty amazing to someone like me who can't even open mine under water in a swimming pool, and I am almost 13.

He said, "The baby has even begun to develop tiny fingernails." I looked at my raggedy ones and decided to quit biting them. I didn't want the baby to come out with a better manicure!

I GUESS all of his comments were necessary, and I was *trying* to keep my mouth shut like I had promised Mama I would, but Dr. Sisler was just prolonging the important part too long.

I was encouraging him to move on by nodding in agreement to every blah-blah thing he said. That's when he uttered the sentence that almost sent me through the ceiling. "I'm ninety-percent sure that you're having a girl."

Hip! Hip! Hooray!

In the video he made for us to take home, I can actually see the heart beating, and in one of the ultrasound pictures, I swear that she is waving at us. Mama put that one on the refrigerator.

Next time, if they do an ultrasound, they will rule out a boy for sure. I just know it!

P.S. Sally was as sore as I was, so every morning we are going to ride laps around the neighborhood, which hopefully will get us in shape before we do another 15-20 mile marathon! My legs couldn't survive another visit from the night gorilla.

Mama says Sally and I should get our lazy bones out of bed before 10:30, so that our rides won't be so hot, but I think she is just interested in squeezing more hours of chores out of me.

"The day's half gone by the time you two get moving!" she said this morning as I dragged myself all the way to the living room where she was watching Dr. Phil.

"Sally and I deserve a break after making it through seventh grade. It was brutal," I said.

"Wait until real life sets in," she said.

What is this that I'm living now? A cartoon?

Friday, June 9

Dear Journal,

Now that Dr. Sisler has made me the happiest big sister on the face of the earth, I can concentrate on the important things in life. First, I only have two months to help Mama and Dad pick out a name. Second, what color paint should we get for the room? Third, shopping! Sally says she will go with me to pick out some baby clothes for my new SISTER!!!

I can't believe what help a best friend is. We must have spent three hours today going through baby name books and decorating magazines. No wonder we are best friends! Our tastes are just the same.

Saturday, June 10

Dear Journal,

Mama has threatened to lock me in my room and nail the door shut until after the baby gets here if I don't stop doing my "sister" dance. "You're annoying your brothers unnecessarily and making both me and the baby nervous with your shenanigans!"

I suspect she is just as happy and dancing on the inside. She was on the phone to her sisters last night for hours. I could tell that they kept suggesting names—not that I was eavesdropping, but Mama kept saying things like, "Alexis? Oh, that is a good one. Wait, I'm not even considering it until I know for 100% sure it's a girl." Then she went on to tell about poor little Jeffrey from the grocery store.

I hope Mama continues to hold strong and doesn't settle on a name before I have a chance to present my list of possibilities! I'm reading the baby name book as fast as I can! Only problem is it's hard to read and DANCE at the same time! Boom-Chicka-Boom!

P.S. Knowing Mama, she has probably decided on a name and just doesn't want her six children making fun of her choice until it's written in stone on the birth certificate.

Nevertheless, soon I will offer my extensive list of possibilities, with the arguments for each choice enumerated!

P.P.S. I wish Katrina would stop by so that I could teach her the sister dance. I bet she would love it, and the two of us together could really irritate the guys.

Sunday, June 11

Dear Journal,

I have been picked on my whole life for my less than melodious name. "Venola" doesn't exactly dance off the tongue, does it? I'm determined not to let my parents do the same thing to the baby.

At first, I thought it might be better to go with something traditional, like Emma or Emily, so that she wouldn't be singled out and asked to spell her name, but I also don't want her to have a name like five other people in her class. This happened in kindergarten—only not to me. We had so many Zachs that the teacher had to attach their last initials, and she made them wear name tags for an extra month just so she could yell at the right one. Eight years later, they still go by Zach B., Zach M., Zach R., and Zach T. We had two Zach B's, but Zach Bender (Zach B2) now goes by his middle name "Bryce."

(I wonder if the Zachs answer when their parents yell without the addition of the last name initials.)

I have highlighted about half the names in the baby name book, but a better idea hit me the other day while Miss Wilma was looking at a gardening catalog. I found some really original ones!

Allium Rose
Bugbane (more of a brother's name) Same thing with "Yucca"!
Cassia Cutright (Too much alliteration?)
Dianthus
Echinacea Sky
Hyacinth
Lavender
Lily Stargazer
Meadow Sage
Rose
Verbena Cutright? Too close to Venola

Violet (I know a whole family of J's.)
Primrose—uppity
Daisy—doesn't sound too bright
Calliopsus
Chrysanthemum could be Chrys
Dusty Miller
Patience

I've narrowed my favorites down to Lily Stargazer, Hyacinth Marie, or Echinacea Sky. How can Mama resist?

I checked all three out to make sure that none of the initials spelled anything disgusting because I know a girl with the initials C.O.W. and a boy Z.I.T. Poor Zach T. What were his parents thinking? He says he was named after his father and grandfather, so I guess ZITS run in his family. Ha.Ha.

I almost changed "Sky" to a "T" middle name like "Taylor," but nothing sounded as beautiful as Echinacea Sky Cutright. However, it would be cool to be "ETC."

P.S. Apparently my sister's name isn't important to Sally. This afternoon, she started banging her head on my desk. "Just pick something. I need some outdoors and sunshine." Did I complain when she bragged for the whole bike ride about all the money she's making at her mother's flower shop this summer? Nooooooooo.

Monday, June 12

Dear Journal,

I gave Mama a highlighter and asked her to mark her three favorites, so that we can compare. After all, I want to be diplomatic because it is her baby, too. However, she is just looking at the list and shaking her head back and forth. I can't tell if she is laughing or crying.

Still Monday, June 12

Dear Journal,

I have my name campaigning work cut out for me because Mama lacks the creative gene and has only highlighted one "remote" possibility from my five-page list.

"Lily's not bad," she said. Then she went back to shaking her head "no." "Absolutely not," she said, when I asked her why she hadn't highlighted the "Stargazer" part. "If it's a pair that can't be broken up, Lily's not even under consideration. I'm sorry, my dear Lavender, but it's back to the drawing board for you." I can't believe she remembers that I used to want to be called a flower name, too! That was ages ago!

P.S. Yikes! Now that I've given Mama at least one name possibility, it's time to concentrate on an immediate major life decision. I'm meeting Sally at DQ after the paper route. Which Blizzard should I have?

P.P.S. I don't think Mama remembers that my cat's middle name is Lily, since we mostly call her "Tiger" now. But that would be cool if she named her baby after my cat. I'm sure Tiger would be honored.

Tuesday, June 13

Dear Journal,

When I delivered Miss Wilma's paper today, she had about 100 skeins of yarn spread out on her couch. "Okay, Miss V, should I go traditional pink and white, or give your new baby sister a special Miss Wilma creation to remember me by?"

I am a Libra and always find it difficult making up my mind, but with this rainbow of yarn, it was impossible. After twenty minutes of putting different color combinations together, and two of my customers calling Miss Wilma's to complain about their non-delivered papers, I admitted decision-making defeat.

Wednesday, June 14

Dear Journal,

"You've got to be kidding! She'll look like a little bumblebee!" I squealed when Sally suggested black and gold.

"Well, my niece dressed up as a bumblebee for Halloween and looked cute," she said with a definite pout in her voice, which was heading quickly towards Huffyville.

I smiled and nodded in my most sincere attempt at faking agreement. It was time to do some repair work to Sally's fashion-deprived ego because summer is still young, and we have a tendency to snip at each other if we spend too much time together. In fact, during previous summers, we've gone weeks without speaking over disagreements that escalated over whether we should split a sundae with sprinkles or nuts.

"You're right, Sally, but this is an everyday blanket—instead of for a special occasion like Halloween. I want something Lily can pass down to her children's children. You know, a family heirloom."

"It's just a blanket. Not the Hope Diamond," she said.

"Yikes!" I said, looking down at my nonexistent watch. "I promised to scrub the kitchen floor before my paper route. Mama can't bend down that far anymore."

P.S. Can a lie be good if it is uttered in order to save a friendship?

P.P.S. What are the odds that Sally will mention the scrubbing floor thing to my mom? Ugh! I know, I better get to scrubbing! Why didn't I make up something fun? Like finishing off the ice cream so that she doesn't gain too much weight!

Thursday, June 15

Dear Journal,

I decided to help Mama with her pregnancy by reading on the Internet. Every suggestion that I make, she torpedoes with either, "Yes, Venola, I have had six children, so I do know a little bit about this," or "That's a lot of wahoo!" which is not very nice since I am using my own valuable time to conduct this research for her.

Just today I told her what I thought was a very good piece of advice. "Babycenter.com says it's a good idea to take a tour of the hospital before your delivery."

Mama cracked up.

"Venola Mae, with six kids, I know every inch of that hospital, and your dad could drive there blindfolded. Now if you want to help this old pregnant woman, how about taking the clothes out of the washer and putting them in the dryer?"

Is that gratitude or what?

Friday, June 16

Dear Journal,

If I don't get some visible appreciation soon, I am going to stop trying to help Mama because it is turning me into Cinderella—the one who works all the time, not the one who gets to go to fancy balls. I read today that beta-carotene is important for the baby's eye development, so I made Mama a carrot slushy.

"Did you have to use *every* carrot in the house?" she barked. "I am intelligent enough to eat properly, Venola Mae Cutright. Stop pestering me!" Then she took my hand, placed it on the handle of the vacuum cleaner, clicked it on, and sat down on the couch with the admittedly giant slushy that I had made her.

Even worse than vacuuming, she made me drink half of the slushy. I think I'm turning orange.

"Carrots don't grow on trees," she snapped when I tried to pour my half down the sink—like I'm an idiot who hasn't watched Bugs Bunny my whole life!

Oh well, if we are fuzzy blobs to the baby when she comes out, it's not my fault. I tried. She's going to think she's seeing double or quadruple anyway when she sees all of her brothers!

Saturday, June 17

Dear Journal,

What *would* my family do without me for entertainment?

Before going to bed, I needed a sandwich, so I made one of my new vegetarian creations. A lettuce, banana pepper, and mayonnaise sandwich on cracked wheat bread. All the ingredients were there, which isn't always the case with four brothers, so I threw it together and headed for the TV.

My mouth was watering as I moved in for the first bite. I chewed and chewed, and then swallowed. Because I had just eaten a piece of candy, or six, I thought my taste buds were making everything taste bitter, but something wasn't right. "Yuck," I said, and spit into my napkin. "The mayonnaise is bad!"

Dad said, "It tasted fine ten minutes ago."

"Well, it's bad now," I said and headed for the trash can.

"You eat that sandwich, Young Lady. I just bought that mayonnaise yesterday," Mama said. "Your eyes are just bigger than your stomach after all those M&M's you've been munching on."

I held the sandwich up to my nose and said, "Here, you try."

Mama bit into the sandwich, and said, "It's a *perfectly* good cabbage sandwich. I'm not sure I would opt for banana peppers, but the mayo is fine!"

"*Cabbage*? I hate cabbage. Isn't that head lettuce?"

That's when they all cracked up. Bobby was tickled more than when I gave him my meatloaf the other night.

"Venola the Vegetarian, my foot!" he said. "She doesn't even know the difference between lettuce and cabbage. You make one heck of a vegetarian, Dumbo!" and then he grabbed my sandwich and finished it in three bites and let fly one of his repulsive burps.

I went to my room, but not before hearing Mama yell at Bobby for calling me names and being ill-mannered. So the evening wasn't a complete fiasco!

Sunday, June 18

Dear Journal,

My parents are tired of me bugging them about a name, so when we were leaving church, they wasted no time accepting Miss Wilma's offer for me to have lunch.

"If you don't think she'll be a bother," Dad said as he ushered/pulled Mama down the church steps and nearly ran to the car. Should I be offended?

Oh well, the sting of my parents' rejection wore off quickly once we arrived at the funeral home. Although we stopped on the stairs to her apartment twice to catch "our breaths," mostly Miss Wilma is acting like her old self. She gossiped about every one of her neighbors while she pulled food out of the frig and reached into the highest cabinets to grab ingredients for the bean and cheese quesadillas. I made lime Kool-Aid and frosted her famous Dream-Whip coconut cake.

When she went to lift a particularly heavy casserole dish out of the hutch, I ran over and said, "Let me get that down for you, Miss Wilma."

"Save that energy to help your poor pregnant mother. I'm not helpless yet," she grouched, which let me know we were back to normal.

"Is your brother coming for lunch?" I asked, hoping to get a look at his socks.

Miss Wilma shook her head. "When he heard the menu, he politely declined. He said beans and funeral directing don't go well together. He has an image to uphold and doesn't want to sound like a helicopter getting ready for take off during a service."

I didn't realize Mr. Facemeir could crack a joke.

"What's with the no-meat menu?" I asked as we sat down.

"Well, it's never too late to start a healthier lifestyle," she said. I was touched, even downright pleased that I could possibly be having an effect on my friend. Then she went on to say, "Plus, I can always drive down and get a Big Mac after you leave."

Monday, June 19

Dear Journal,

FINALLY Katrina picked up all she wanted from her room, so I can officially start my migration. Dad said, "Don't get too comfortable. She'll probably be back before your new paint dries."

Does that seem fair to you? If I spend all my time redecorating, why should Katrina get to swoop back down and reap the benefits of my hard work and creative ability?

Sally came over and helped me clean up what piggy left behind. Katrina said, "You can have anything I left," which sounded good until I realized she only left some yucky country CD's that are scratched, an ugly asphalt-gray bedspread, a broken book shelf, a whole bunch of candy WRAPPERS, and about two inches of dust.

The worst part is she took her full-sized bed and matching nightstand, so I will have to bribe my brothers to help me drag my twin down the hallway. For now, the room is completely empty, except for ugly gray walls and a purple stain the size of a Frisbee right in the center of the even uglier gray carpet. Katrina definitely spent every penny of her paychecks on clothing instead of interior design.

After we scrubbed the best we could, Sally and I sat down on the floor and shared a well-deserved Dr. Pepper with lots of ice.

"This room looks like a bad mood," Sally said.

No arguments here. I agreed completely. "It reminds me of a school bus splashing you with grimy freezing slush."

"On a windy March morning," she added. Then her eyes got as big as silver dollars. "What if this room's why your sister was always so grouchy?" Sally asked, which made sense because since Katrina moved out, she's always smiling and nice to the whole family.

"Maybe *you'll* morph into cranky Katrina if you move in without checking the chi," Sally said without smiling. "I suggest a major *fung schway* before you move your stuff in here just to be on the safe side."

Sally and her mom watch HGTV all the time, so she knows more about decorating than I do, but I didn't want to appear stupid, so I just agreed and figured I could look it up on the Internet later.

Tuesday, June 20

Dear Journal,

Even though it sounds like "fung schway," it's really spelled "feng shui," and so it took me quite a while to figure out what Sally meant about decorating my room. According to the websites, my room might have negative energy that will bring me bad luck. I'm more confused than ever. I hope Sally has time to help feng shui my room before we leave for camp. (Yes, I'm leaving Bobby in charge of my paper route, and all of my profits, plus $15.00 extra, which I don't want to think about or I will get sick.)

Miss Wilma says feng shui is a "bunch of hooey," but I'm not taking any chances. Maybe that's why I had the pain in my leg. What if it is negative energy from having my bed pointing in the wrong direction instead of just a silly old muscle cramp?

Wednesday, June 21

Dear Journal,

Wow. It's a good thing Mama wouldn't let me put the family computer in my room because according to this feng shui website, electronics can sabotage a "peaceful atmosphere."

Sally and I went to the library and checked out all three of their feng shui books. Now we are *both* more confused than ever. Sally doesn't know much more about the stuff than I do, even though she wouldn't admit it under the worst possible night gorilla torture.

We worked all afternoon making sketches of possible layouts for my room. She left mad because I told her no way was I sleeping with my bed turned diagonally in the room with a vase of fresh cut flowers on a table behind my head. Just because her mom can bring home flowers from the shop anytime she wants, doesn't mean I can afford to live *The Lifestyle of the Rich and Famous* on a paper route budget. Also, the bed turned in that weird direction would take up most of the space, and I wouldn't have room for the oversized chair that Miss Wilma says I can have. It will be perfect for curling up and reading in.

It's my room—not Sally's! Shouldn't I get the final say? Even though we're friends, we couldn't BE more different.

Thursday, June 22

Dear Journal,

Okay, placing my bed was easy. It had to go on the north wall because for some ancient Chinese reason, I can't put it on the wall that has a window or on the wall next to the bathroom. Also, my feet can't point towards the door because that is bad luck, too. Apparently that's the way they carry dead bodies out. Gross.

Hey, since my luck isn't always the best, and I'm always broke, I'm willing to try anything. So if the books say I need a specific wealth corner, who am I to argue? In my Wealth/Abundance NW corner, I am going to put my dresser with my money-colored lava lamp and piggy bank on top. Since there is a window there, I don't want all my good energy drifting out, so I will hang a lucky crystal if I can buy one cheap. I better ask Bobby about which direction is which because if I mix them up, will I be jinxed and even more broke than when I started? (If this is even possible!)

According to the library books, red is important in feng shui, but it gives me the creeps, so I am just going to use a little bit. In the Fame part of my room (North), I'll hang my Paper Carrier of the Month Certificates in red frames. Then I will have my bed right underneath my achievements, and it will make me dream of future successes. I hope!

Is bright yellow an okay color for a bedspread, or will I get sick of it in a week? According to the feng shui color chart, "yellow energy is related to the ability to understand." I always sit on my bed to do my homework, so if yellow boosts my brain power and brings up my grades, my parents will probably spring for the new comforter!

In the Love (NE) corner, I will put my nightstand with a good reading-in-bed lamp, and maybe some pictures of my friends and me doing the monkey dance and riding our bikes on the trail. I have a cute photo of Sammy pretending to kiss a cow, but I don't want people thinking I am in love with him, or the cow, so I will have to keep it in a drawer.

Miss Wilma's old brown chair will be perfect in the Creative/ Children (East) section of the room. I saw a soft orange throw at Wal-Mart that I can toss over it. If orange really does make for a "happy, creative environment," count me in. Mama will probably give me an ultrasound picture until we have some color photos of the baby. Or if she would HURRY UP and GET HERE, I could start a sister collage. I'm going to keep a basket of my friends' picture books by the chair and read to the baby when we can't sleep!

Feng shui has made me feng tired.

Friday, June 23

Dear Journal,

Katrina took Sally and me shopping. Mama's feet were swelling, so she opted for our couch and the remote. Oh well, she would have keeled over with a heart attack if she'd seen all my purchases. Katrina suggested that I might want to break Mama in gradually to my new things to keep her from yelling. I found a crystal, the ultimate sunshine yellow bedspread and curtains, four neon throw pillows in blue, indigo, red, and green, and my orange fuzzy throw for the chair.

I wasn't completely selfish. I also bought Sally and Katrina lunch at Wendy's, and Tiger a white sheepskin window seat that attaches to the window sill. It will be perfect in the Family/Pet Quadrant of my room, right next to the rack with Grandma's quilt. Tiger's going to love watching the birds outside!

P.S. I will officially be delivering papers now until I am 110 years old. I had to borrow $20 from Katrina to finish my extravaganza, which once I go to the bank and pay her back will officially clean out my savings and my piggy bank will be starving until collection day.

P.P.S. When we got home, Katrina helped me hang the curtains and put on the bedspread. She said, "It looks a hundred times better than when it was my room!" I was afraid she might be trying to say she wanted it back, but I don't think there's any chance of that. She seemed in a rush to get back to her own life, even though I begged her to stay for supper. Things are different with just brothers.

Saturday, June 24

Dear Journal,

Where in the world am I supposed to find a statue of a laughing Buddha? According to these feng shui books, if I rub his big belly each day, supposedly it will bring me luck. Is that why Mama's big belly has turned into such a hand magnet?

The Buddhas online cost $86.95. Do banks lend money with bicycles as collateral?

Sunday, June 25

Dear Journal,

My Wealth and Prosperity corner just got a little more prosperous! Can feng shui possibly work this fast?

This morning, I was telling Mama about Buddha's belly and chasing her around the kitchen rubbing her belly, while she swatted me away with a newspaper.

Five hours later, here I am placing my own gorgeous teakwood Buddha on the dresser. Magic? Nah. Just Miss Wilma, whose picture is definitely going on my southeast closet door under "Helpful People"!

She said, "Johnny sent the little tubby guy to me from Asia when he was in the military."

"You're giving it to me? Won't your brother get mad?" I asked.

"Not if he doesn't find out. Stick it in your paperbag," she said, giving it a final wrap with a paper towel. "He'd just stick it in a closet like I did, where it would never see daylight again, or even worse he'd humiliate Buddha by putting a big old number on him."

Miss Wilma laughs like no other. And her laughter is a better sound than the ice cream truck on a hot day, which I hear now! Later, Journal!

P.S. I found the ideal Miss Wilma picture in one of my miscellaneous junk boxes. She is sitting on the bleachers at the county fair with a Wal-Mart bag on her head to keep her hair out of the rain. It captures her "I don't care what anyone else thinks" personality perfectly!

Monday, June 26

Dear Journal,

I made my wish on Buddha's belly as soon as I woke up. I wonder if belly wishes are like birthday wishes and won't come true if I tell you? Let's just say if all goes as planned, Buddha's previous owner will be around for a long, long time. And not just because she gives fantastic presents!

If I had to pick a best friend, would it be Miss Wilma or Sally? Let's hope this isn't a truth or dare question at camp next week! Miss Wilma never makes fun of my taste. I think my colorful room is every bit as beautiful as Missy's, but Sally took one look at the finished product and rolled her eyes!

Then she rolled them again when she saw Buddha on the dresser. When I told her the story behind it, she said, "A little shui goes a long way. Don't make me start calling you, 'Venola, The Granola! The vegetarian thing is weird enough." Who died and made her Queen of Design or My Diet? And do I criticize her disgusting animal eating addiction? Well, once maybe. Or twice. But still!

Tuesday, June 27

Dear Journal,

I am not going to camp after all. Sally thinks it is because we aren't getting along very well, but the main reason is I am broke. I can't help that I got carried away shopping and didn't save enough to pay my extortionist of a brother. I didn't want to admit this because Sally has said enough rude things about my room renovations, so I told her that Mama needed my help around the house.

Wednesday, June 28

Dear Journal,

Everyone leaves for camp in two days. I spent hours, okay weeks, laying out what I was taking and now I'm half sick to be putting it back away.

Dad stuck his head around my door and said, "Thanks for thinking of your mother, Kiddo." Somehow I think they have the idea I am staying home because I'm worried about her. Did Sally call and try to convince them to change their minds about me going to camp?

Oh well, whatever the reason, Mama has suggested that I have my friends over tomorrow night for pizza and a last-minute slumber party before they leave. If I did, would Missy make fun of my house? It's nothing like hers!

Thursday, June 29

Dear Journal,

They are coming! Missy, Sally, Karla, and Precious! I have no idea where they are going to sleep. Maybe we can push the bed against the wall and stretch out on sleeping bags.

Gotta go. They will be here in less than five hours. Brownies to bake!

Friday, June 30

Dear Journal,

Martha Stewart watch out! My party was a major success. When Missy walked in, she said my room was "Funky with a capital F." And she meant it in a good way! I could just tell by the way she took in every little detail. She said, "I didn't know you had such an eye for color." Then a little later, she said, "I wish I had a sister to take me shopping. Decorators never let you pick anything out for yourself." Can you believe it? She didn't even seem the least bit upset that I didn't have a maid or a phone in my bathroom. Besides my "fab" sense of design, as Karla called it, my house had something all three girls liked even better. Four teenage brothers. Tee hee. My friends didn't mind that the apes ate most of the cheese pizzas we made!

Bobby came outside and played hide-n-seek with us girls, which made Missy's night because she confessed to me that she is in "love, love, love with him." I have a major confession of my own. I might not be a true vegetarian anymore. While we were running around outside, the gnats were so thick that I couldn't breathe without swallowing or inhaling quite a few. Do insects count as meat? It was totally involuntary consumption!

I'm back on the vegetarian wagon now.

P.S. When my friends and I were getting ready for bed, I'm not sure why, but I told them about Mr. Facemeir's socks. Everyone laughed so loud that Bobby banged on the wall and wanted to know what was so funny, which made us laugh even harder. Missy said they should grab up Facemeirs' Funeral Home as their camp sponsor, and if they can get it, they are going to number their uniform socks in honor of Mr. Facemeir.

"I don't think any team picked Facemeirs' last year, so it shouldn't be a problem," Sally said. "Our slogan can be 'We'll die trying!'"

Missy said, "No, let's do 'Drop dead, you other teams!'"

Then I remembered what Miss Wilma always teased her brother he should use in his advertisements: "We bury the competition."

Karla even looked up from her *Bride* magazine to laugh at this one. Now I really wish I were going with them.

P.P.S. Precious was a perfect houseguest. He didn't chase Tiger Lily, and I warned my whole family not to feed him people food.

Saturday, July 1

Dear Journal,

I stopped in to tell Miss Wilma about the party and gave her the brownie I saved back for her. I thought she might be jealous that I had so much fun without her, but instead she seemed as happy as can be to hear every, well almost every, party detail.

Of course her favorite part was the possibility of my friends numbering their socks.

"Do you think Mr. Facemeir would be mad if he found out?" I asked.

"Are you kidding? He'd take it as an extreme compliment," she said.

P.S. I guess I should have saved two brownies because she gave me the biggest part of the one I took her. Yum!

Sunday, July 2

Dear Journal,

Since when is offering interior decorating advice pestering
someone? People on *Trading Spaces* seem happy when someone
offers free advice.

I was just trying to finish the baby's room before she gets here.
I mean, my parents yell when I tell them there's plenty of time
to finish my homework on the way to school. Well, as far as I'm
concerned, Mama and the baby are on the bus, and they're nearing
the school. No time to waste!

Where is the baby going to sleep? Should we put the bed facing
North, etc.? You know, feng shui for babies.

Mama said, "Let me finish my nap. We have months to consider
all this. The baby will sleep in a crib next to us for the first month or
so."

If this is the case, why did I waste my $34.95 on a baby monitor?

P.S. I should have taken out a loan from the Bank of Bobby and
gone to camp. I wonder if Sally and the gang have already Saran-
wrapped the counselor's toilet. I can't believe I'm missing out!

Monday, July 3

Dear Journal,

Mama had a migraine, which NO, I did not cause like my dad accused. To the contrary, being the thoughtful daughter that I am, I fixed supper while she stretched out with an ice pack on her head.

"Not more alfalfa sprouts and tofu patties," Bobby whined when he saw me cooking. Ha.Ha.

Yummy black beans, rice, and cheddar-jalapeño cornbread shut him right up. The whole gang liked my spinach salad, too. The only complaint during the whole meal was Dad saying that carrots would have made the salad better and helped his tired eyes. Since he looked at Mama and winked, I'm thinking he was teasing. Just in case, I got even by offering him the last eight ounces of my old carrot slushy that *somehow* had gotten scooted to the back of the fridge. He quieted right down when the boys started double daring him to drink it. Brothers can be quite helpful sometimes. Tee hee!

Tuesday, July 4

Dear Journal,

My brothers and sister were all scheduled to work, so no real picnic. Dad grilled, and everyone ate when they wandered in. This used to be my favorite holiday, especially the grilled hot dogs! I ate corn and watermelon.

P.S. Miss Wilma and I set off a few firecrackers behind the funeral home, but we had to stop after the third one because her brother stuck his head out the back door and complained.

Wednesday, July 5

Dear Journal,

I started making a hospital list for Mama, even though she said that the hospital provides almost everything.

"I'll just have your Dad grab a nightgown and robe on our way out the door," she said. My mouth fell open a mile wide. Hasn't she noticed Dad is color and fashion blind?

"I'll agree to Dad driving you, but I can't let him be in charge of something as important as your labor wardrobe," I said.

"Trust me," Mama said, "at that particular moment, I won't care about my wardrobe."

I insisted that it was no trouble. "Can I help it if I want you to be completely comfortable during your unfortunate confinement?"

"Daughter, I am going to the hospital, not to death row," she said.

Mama laughs at me all the time, but I bet she will be down-on-her-knees grateful when she is in her boring sterile hospital room, and I pop in and surprise her with not only all the essential toiletries like a toothbrush and shampoo, but a special care package with apple-pie scented candles, watermelon-scented hand lotion, strawberry lip moisturizer, barrettes for her hair, Doritos (to offer guests if she can't have food), a picture of her six lovely children so she'll remember that the pain is worth it, word search and crossword puzzles, the latest *People* magazine and *TV Guide*, and a boom box with a special V.M.C. mix CD. If she is nice to me, I might even throw in my Gameboy. She will feel so pampered she might never want to come home!

P.S. When she saw me trying to squeeze a tennis ball and rolling pin into the hospital bag, she said, "What in the world are those for?" I should have known what her reaction would be, but the Internet said they were good for back massages during labor.

She insisted they come out, but I sneaked the ball back in because I figure it could come in handy in the waiting room if I get bored. My brothers are always up for a game of indoor ball.

P.P.S. So far I have twenty-five handpicked labor songs on the CD, including "Babe" by Styx, "Baby, Baby" by Amy Grant, "Baby, Baby, Baby" by Pretty Boy, and "Baby, Baby, Baby, Baby, Ooh Baby" by De La Soul. Even though I used to like "Hit Me Baby One More Time" by Britney Spears, I left it off because the baby doesn't need any more encouragement to kick us. She's violent enough already. Plus, Mama always turns the radio off when the song comes on, and after all, the CD *is* for her. I threw in "Born in the U.S.A." for Dad because he loves Springsteen, and I don't want him to feel totally left out!

P.P.P.S. *If* I have time, maybe I can make Dad his very own "driving to the hospital" CD. "Born to Be Wild" by Steppenwolf always makes him drive a little faster.

Thursday, July 6

Dear Journal,

Mama was sitting on the couch reading when I went to the kitchen for a drink.

"What are you doing up past twelve?" I asked, because she and Dad usually fall asleep in front of the TV if they aren't in bed by ten.

"Isn't the *mother* supposed to ask that question?" she said, reaching for my glass of orange juice.

"I'm reading the *best* mystery ever, and I've only got two more chapters," I said. Mama has always been pretty lenient about letting me stay up late if I want to read, as long as it's not a school night.

"I wish I could concentrate long enough to read a *paragraph*," she said, putting her book down and rubbing her belly, "but this little one has her nights and days mixed up. Right when I'm settling down for the night, she's just getting going. She's definitely related to you."

"Hey, what do you mean by that?" I asked, not sure if I should be offended.

"I'm just saying you were the most active child in Cutright history, that is, until now. So if your current energy level is any indication of how this child will turn out, I've got my job cut out for me."

Okay. Now I am offended. Plus, she drank all my juice.

P.S. Mama just said "HER." Hooray for baby girls!

Friday, July 7

Dear Journal,

Tonight was a total mother/daughter evening. Dad came straight home from work, grabbed a sandwich and my brothers, and they loaded up the pickup and left to mow yards. They've been running this little business since my brothers were old enough to help out. Then they use the money for buying manly things like hunting supplies or fishing gear, which I don't think is quite fair. Even though I'm older than the boys were when they started mowing, my dad says stuff like, "Why don't you help your mom? You'd just get hurt." Of course, the boys all stick their tongues out and wave as the truck pulls away. How immature! No one would ever guess that *I* am the youngest.

This time, it was almost worth the discrimination, just to be alone with Mama. I've never really valued these evenings because I am always so mad at the male members of my family for leaving me behind, but now that we are about ready to have an intruder on our evenings, I'm treasuring them a little. I polished Mama's toenails with the new crackle technique I learned at Missy's party. I had to describe the process to her since she can't see her feet anymore. Ha. Ha.

Then we walked around the neighborhood with only minor neighbor interruptions. After that, I propped her swollen but nicely pedicured feet up on a throw pillow, and we watched a Julia Roberts marathon.

Since Mama has been told to watch her weight, I didn't tempt her with our regular Dairy Queen trip—even though I wanted it really, really bad. Instead I made us both healthy Venola Mae milkshakes.

"Not very big," she yelled from the couch, obviously reliving the carrot slushy disaster. No such worry. She loved it! I blended strawberries, frozen yogurt, and skim milk, just like Miss Wilma said.

P.S. Dr. Sisler would be quite pleased with his little protégé!

164

Saturday, July 8

Dear Journal,

Okay, I've had enough mother/daughter quality time! Mama is still having trouble sleeping, which makes her tired and cranky. I wish I could mow with the guys instead of hanging with her. I heard her telling Dad she was having a few false labor pains. How does she know they are false?

Dad said, "Maybe I shouldn't go. The boys can do the three yards we have scheduled," which gave me a chance to stick my tongue out at them. Ha.Ha.

"I've probably got another month. Scram," she said, waving her hand.

So now I am in charge of a woman who might go into labor any minute.

When we went for our walk, I said, "Are you having a pain?" so many times that she threatened to sprint home without me.

She is also mad because I called Dr. Sisler. "Don't bother the man at home," she said.

He said that I'm a good daughter to worry and just to make sure she takes warm baths and drinks lots of liquids. It feels like I am babysitting my mother. Weird!

Sunday, July 9

Dear Journal,

I guess the labor was a false alarm because Mama is okay, and we all went to church. She just had one little meltdown before getting in the van.

"My rings won't go on," she said, shoving with all her might. Dad tried to reassure her, but she just started back towards the house. "People might think we're having trouble," she said and blew her nose.

I couldn't believe she was crying, but Dad didn't help the situation a bit. He told her no one would even notice her hands or rings, which of course she thought was because she was so fat. Dad told the rest of us who were standing outside the van with our mouths hanging open, "Get in. Your mother's just a little more emotional right now," which wasn't a bright thing to say when she was already upset.

Surely my parents won't get a divorce with number seven on the way—will they?

Monday, July 10

Dear Journal,

Things are still cranky around the house, and I miss having Sally to escape with on the bike trail. I rode out to the dairy farm, but not even the cows were outside to talk to me. Are they taking naps, too? Miss Wilma is resting a lot more this summer, but she insists that she is "as fine as can be." What does this really mean?

Nothing more to write.

Tuesday, July 11

Dear Journal,

    I am so bored that I offered to make supper so that Mama can elevate her legs. Since she had already thawed out hamburger and she didn't want me to waste it, Bobby agreed to fry them. I have always hated the squishing sound and slimy feeling of making it into patties. I should have become a vegetarian years ago. Yuck.

    P.S. I never thought Bobby would volunteer to do anything in the kitchen. Could he be turning into a nice person? Gulp. Did I just write that?

    P.P.S. Mama is not wearing her rings. Hope it's just the weight gain.

Wednesday, July 12

Dear Journal,

I can't breathe. Is Mama too old to have a baby? I found an article on the Internet that says Mama is "high-risk" because she is 39. Will she be okay? Could she die? I thought that only happened in olden times like on *Little House on the Prairie*. Could my sister be in danger? After all, Mama has lost a baby before. I'm afraid to talk to her because I don't want to worry her, and she has forbidden me to call Dr. Sisler any more. Help!

P.S. I tried to call Katrina, but she and Cindy are never home.

Thursday, July 13

Dear Journal,

I finally couldn't keep my fears inside any longer. "I'm in perfect health," Mama reassured me. "Listen, since you did such a great job on my emergency hospital bag, could you make two more?"

At first, I thought she wanted me to pack one for me so that I could go in the delivery room with her, which made my knees weak with fear, but then she said, "Why shouldn't your dad and baby sister have Venola bags, too?"

Is she just trying to take my mind off other things?

I've been trying to find Internet lists of stuff that dads need in the hospital, but they are limited. One site recommended a bathing suit, but I don't think Mama is going to give Dad permission to sneak off and go swimming.

Dad's list:
Toothpaste, razor, and shampoo
Money for parking
Money for his children to borrow for vending machines
Snacks
Deodorant (He sweats like no other!)
Video camera (Mama says NO WAY!)

P.S. I can't finish packing the baby's bag because Katrina has to go shopping with me. I want to buy something special for the coming home outfit!!!

P.P.S. Mama says the swimming trunks are probably so Dad won't get wet if he has to help her out of the tub or shower. "That's the least of my concerns," she said. "Pack extra deodorant for him instead." Told you!

Friday, July 14

Dear Journal,

My brothers and I offered to treat my parents to dinner and a movie before the baby gets here. They just stared at us suspiciously.

Dad looked at Mama and said, "Would you rather rent a movie and send the kids to Pizza Hut?"

Mama nodded. "I'll rest better not worrying about objects whizzing around my living room, or who has whom in a sleeper hold."

Do they know their children or what?

P.S. They also have memories like elephants. Dad told me to take it easy on the peppers. Very funny!

P.P.S. Why *do* my brothers love wrestling so much?

Saturday, July 15

Dear Journal,

Since my friends are still at camp, I think Miss Wilma sensed my boredom and asked if I wanted to spend the night, but I figured I better stay near the house since the guys were mowing again. After all, I've got less than a month to be Mama's youngest daughter. What will it be like not to be the baby anymore?

Sunday, July 16

Dear Journal,

There is absolutely nothing to do. I'm *almost* ready to wish for school to start back. Not quite! I was reading one of Mama's pamphlets during a commercial, and it said babies at this stage of development can see. Their eyes are open, and they can follow light.

So I started shining a flashlight on Mama's belly and talking to the baby. "Come on, Lily. Follow the light."

Mama said, "If it is true, how would you like to be rudely awakened by someone shining a bright light in *your* eyes?"

Bobby volunteered to stay awake and shine a light in mine for her. I am putting a chair up against the doorknob tonight just in case he was serious.

Monday, July 17

Dear Journal,

    My leg hurts this morning because I forgot about the Bobby trap and bumped my leg on the chair when I got up to use the bathroom. When I tried to blame Bobby for the scrape on my leg, Mama yelled at me for setting up a fire hazard in my own room. Some days I should just stay in bed.

Tuesday, July 18

Dear Journal,

I have been reading picture books to Mama's belly so the baby will love books as much as I do. My reading teacher said that you should add some razzle-dazzle to your reading voice, so for tonight's performance of *Five Little Monkeys Jumping on the Bed*, I added a few bed jumps and falls. I thought I turned a mere picture book into a one woman show, and I expected rave reviews, but Mama said, "If you are going to continue these night-time readings, you're going to have to take them down a notch. The baby kicked for an hour and a half after last night's rap rendition of *Chicka Chicka Boom Boom*, and another reading like that monkey book might just jar me into labor."

Critics! If the baby grows up to think books are boring, it won't be my fault!

Wednesday, July 19

Dear Journal,

It's a conspiracy! Society tries to keep baby girls in the "sugar and spice and everything nice" mold by making all their clothes pale pink. Yuck. It's bad enough that it's my gemstone. Every present that the baby has received is pink, and Mama and Katrina are hypnotized by the color. They "oohed and awwwed" over every single pink object in three different stores.

"I refuse to spend even a penny on pink! I hate it!" I gagged when Katrina held up the tenth frilly pink dress.

"That's why you threw up on every single outfit I put on you," Mama said. "It was a fashion statement instead of an upset stomach."

While she was being disgusting, I spotted the ultimate—pale bluejean bibs with flowers on the front pocket and a lavender tee-shirt. If it were in my size, I'd wear it!

Too bad the flowers aren't lilies.

Thursday, July 20

Dear Journal,

I had a long overdue letter from Sally! Their team tee-shirts won first place. Since I was the one who came up with their "Bury the Competition" slogan, they made me an honorary member, and they sent me a shirt. On the front, Sally drew the Grim Reaper playing ping-pong with paddles in both hands, and Missy's picture on the back showed him laughing maniacally and spraying shaving cream on kids. Now I miss going to camp even more!

Friday, July 21

Dear Journal,

I was a little offended that Miss Wilma didn't wait until I finished narrowing down my yarn choices, but she said, "I wanted to get the afghan to your mother before the baby started first grade." She used all of my favorites—lavender, mint green, yellow, baby blue—in a zigzag pattern.

It will look great with the little bluejean outfit that I've talked Mama into bringing the baby home in.

Saturday, July 22

Dear Journal,

I asked Mama if she had any control over the baby's due date.

"Why? Do you have an important date on August 17?" she asked.

"No, but it's extremely important that you hold off until September first. Peridot looks like lime Jello, and you don't want to saddle the baby with that as a birthstone. Sapphire is so much prettier."

When she stopped laughing, she said, "I doubt you have a thing to worry about. All of my children were at least 10 days late, so the baby will probably sidestep this critical obstacle."

Relieved, I headed down the hallway to my room, "And another thing," she yelled after me, "quit calling the baby 'Lily'! Your dad and I haven't made a final decision." Since she was ironing, which I despise doing, I didn't turn around to do any extra convincing. Sorry, Lily, but sometimes you just have to hide if you know what's good for you. I'll teach you all about it.

P.S. Sally's latest letter said that everyone in her cabin had to run laps because they carried the counselor's bed outside with her sleeping in it. I can't believe I'm missing out!

Sunday, July 23

Dear Journal,

Why didn't I go to camp? I could be having a water balloon fight!
There's nothing to do here.

Monday, July 24

Dear Journal,

Mama is having false labor pains again, so I am mom-sitting while the guys mow the Concord Cemetery. Mama and I fixed a picnic this afternoon and planned to ride out into the country with them, but at the last minute, she decided a nap was a better idea.

"You go ahead," she said, because she knows I love to sit in this giant maple tree up on a hill and daydream and write. "You can put the new flowers on Mother and Daddy's graves for me," she said.

I shook my head. "It's too hot," I said, "and anyway, it gets me back late for my paper route."

P.S. My brothers are going to be disappointed when they find out I repossessed the chocolate-chip cookies that I packed in the picnic basket. There was no time to divide them out, and if I hadn't grabbed them, they would have eaten them all without even thinking twice about saving the baker one or two. Tee hee.

Later Monday, July 24

Dear Journal,

I have just experienced my first ambulance ride, and I am now sitting in the waiting room of the hospital while Dr. Sisler examines Mama.

This afternoon, when I realized that the false labor might be true, I wanted to call Miss Wilma, or Sally's mom, or Mr. Bookout, but Mama vetoed them all, "Do NOT call any neighbors, friends, friend's moms, or teachers to take me to the hospital. Your dad will be back soon, and then we'll decide whether it's time to go."

"Even though I got an A in general science, I'm not delivering the baby," I said, lifting Dad's and the baby's bags on one shoulder, and Mama's on the other. I made it halfway down the hallway before collapsing. Then, I dragged them the rest of the way to the front door.

"You aren't going to have to deliver anything but your papers. I always have about 36 hours in the hospital. Trust me. I'm an expert at this. My children are slowpokes from the get-go, and my due date is more than three weeks away."

"I read that only five percent of women actually give birth on their due—"

"Listen you Internet nut, go read a young adult book, and I'll call you if I need a strawberry smoothie in a couple of hours."

So there I was in my room, trying to decide who I could call that wasn't on my mother's forbidden list. Of course, Katrina and Cindy didn't answer even though I tried at least ten times. Then it hit me, Mama didn't say anything about lunch ladies! I called Mrs. Isner, and she said that she had planned to drop off some of her children's old baby stuff sometime, so she might as well "casually" stop by today.

By the time she arrived, Mama was reconsidering waiting so long. Mrs. Isner said, "I'm sort of a nervous driver. Maybe we better call an ambulance just to be safe," so that is how I ended up sitting in the waiting room next to the school cafeteria cook.

P.S. I hope Dad sees the giant notes I left him on the refrigerator, the bathroom door, and right next to the remote. I tried to put them in the places that he would see first.

P.P.S. When I called Katrina from the hospital, she answered on the second ring. Do you think she has Caller ID and has been avoiding my calls? I don't call *that* much. Oh well, she is on her way now!

Tuesday, July 25

Dear Journal,

What a long night! Dad came to the hospital all smelly, so it is a good thing that I packed him a bag. My grass-stained brothers stood around the bed quietly, staring at the floor or out the window, and after a few minutes, James said, "I should put away the mowers before it rains." Could they be afraid like me and just not know how to help?

Mama wasn't completely wrong about how much time she would be in labor. It has already been twenty-four hours. James drove the rest of us kids home last night, but no one slept or argued much, and we didn't even eat all of the pizza that Katrina brought over. Katrina watched scary movies with us, and she French-braided my hair before falling asleep on the couch. But I still didn't sleep very well. In fact, I don't think anyone did.

We were all up, dressed, and back in the waiting room by nine. My brothers are being very odd. You could almost call them polite and considerate. This is scarier than Mama moaning and groaning.

Since Katrina had to leave for work, I've spent the whole evening sitting in Mama's room. My brothers have taken over the waiting room and turned it into ESPN central. The nurses let me stay in with her as much as I want, and they said that if Mama doesn't mind, any or all of us can stay for the delivery, but there are certain things I'm just not ready for. I felt like a wimp, until Miss Wilma said she is not old enough to witness that kind of miracle either.

P.S. Can you believe Bobby volunteered to deliver my papers for me? For FREE? I had completely forgotten about them.

Tuesday, July 25, 11:11 p.m.

Dear Journal,

It is official. I am a big sister! Mama was right and is having fun telling everyone that her labor took exactly thirty-six hours from the time her contractions started. When I went in to see her at around ten-thirty, she was in so much pain that I actually said a prayer, "Please let Mama and the baby be okay. It doesn't matter if it's a boy or a girl. Just hurry up and let it get here healthy."

For that one moment, I understood Mama's comment, "A baby is a baby." However, I AM SURE GLAD TO HAVE A SISTER!!! My brothers backed up flat against the wall and refused to hold her, but not me! I was first in line and didn't let go until Katrina threatened to withhold future pizzas. She says the guys are afraid of dropping the baby. Wimps!

P.S. I can't wait to write Sally. Why don't they have email at camp?

P.P.S. I have a feeling my new sister has great taste. I bet she came early because she hates peridot, just like me. Ruby is so much prettier to have as a birthstone!

Birth Announcement

For the *Elkins Exponent*

By Venola Mae Cutright, Paper Route Carrier and Part-time Journalist

On July 25 at 11:11 p.m., Lily Rose Cutright popped into the world with a fully working set of bionic lungs, which I swear I heard clear out in the waiting room. Lily's brothers, who were busy fighting over which channel to watch, say it is impossible that I heard Lily being born because of the extremely long hallway and TWO sets of heavy-duty double doors. If they are right, and I am wrong, then you better move this announcement to the front page and call it "Psychic Sisters Discovered in Belington!"

Lily Rose is a Cutright through and through—not much hair, bright blue eyes, and a chin that you could harpoon a good-sized catfish on. Yes, we come out pointy. I would tell you her weight, but a lady doesn't like to have that revealed at any age. Let's just say that when she's in your arms, you sure know she's there, but you don't mind one bit because she's a real snuggler and not stinky at all—very often. Ha.Ha.

Mother and daughter are doing well and recovering at their residence on Wabash Avenue. In lieu of gifts, please stop by with a covered dish (preferably vegetarian). The brothers of Lily Rose have already cleaned out what Mrs. Cutright froze in advance, and the sisters are having trouble keeping up with the boys' stomachs.

If you'd like to see Lily Rose's beautiful eyes, it's best to stop by between midnight and 5 a.m. as she's definitely a night owl. Her mama's not feeling the same enthusiasm for the nightlife, so you might want to call first.

Wednesday, July 26

Dear Journal,

In the last few months, my life has completely changed. I am now a feng-shuied vegetarian, who has a baby sister right down the hallway to cuddle any time I want. I've experienced some scares that make me value my friends even more than I did before. In fact, I've made a few extras, including my ex-arch-nemesis Missy. She's even considering becoming a vegetarian with me.

I know people thought that the vegetarian thing was a phase, but I AM a vegetarian and plan to be one for the rest of my life. Holding Lily makes me value living things more than ever.

As far as ever choosing a vegan way of life, I'm not so sure. I do love Dairy Queen, and as I told Missy in science class, it's up to the individual. We have to live with our own consciences. (I still wish I could pronounce this word.)

My decision to stop being a meat eater might not make a big impact on the world, like starting a national vegetarian newsletter or leading a no-meat sitdown strike at school. But if I keep cooking a couple of vegetarian meals a week for my family, I'm saving at least a whole herd of cattle from my brothers, until I come up with a major Ghandi-like approach to get the rest of the world to stop animal violence.

And speaking of my wonderfully supportive family unit, I have it on good authority THAT CERTAIN BROTHERS BET about how many days I would remain a vegetarian.

I *could* have tattled about their gambling, but I have kept it to myself—so far. Maybe if they return the good will, some day we will actually like hanging out with each other like Miss Wilma and Mr. Facemeir. Hey, we didn't kill each other while Mama was in the hospital. That's a start.

As for writing in you, Journal, the entries might be few and far between. I'm going to be busy around the house for a while. So until next time, signing off! I have a sister to spoil. Yahoo!